THE KINGS MARKET KILLER

An enthralling murder mystery with a twist

FRANCES LLOYD

Detective Inspector Jack Dawes Mystery Book 6

JOFFE BOOKS

First published in Great Britain 2020
Joffe Books, London
www.joffebooks.com

Join our mailing list and become one of 1,000s of readers enjoying free Kindle crime thriller, detective, mystery, and romance books and new releases. Receive your first bargain book this month!

www.joffebooks.com

We love to hear from our readers! Please email any feedback you have to: feedback@joffebooks.com

ISBN 978-1-78931-570-7

PROLOGUE

*This world's a city full of straying streets, and death's the market-place
where each one meets.*

        William Shakespeare, *The Two Noble Kinsmen*

You can buy just about anything from the Kings Market. On Saturdays and Sundays, colourful stalls spring up around the market square and overflow into the high street. It's vibrant, noisy and crammed with local artisans, plying their goods. At the high end, there are antiques, craft ales, vintage fashion and gourmet food, catering mainly for the fancies of the well-heeled. The lower end deals in cheap clothes, alternative music and global street food. Here, the unwary shopper might acquire items of dubious provenance and occasional bouts of food poisoning. In the middle, are the butchers, fishmongers, florists and greengrocers that are the lifeblood of an outdoor market.

    Originally, it was known as the Richington Market and was little more than a country fair on a piece of waste ground, known as Richington Green. It had remained like that for much of the eighteenth and nineteenth centuries, with peasants bartering all kinds of wares, including livestock. In 1830, as homage to the accession of benevolent William IV over his dissolute elder brother, George IV, it became known as the Kings Market. Now, nearly two hundred years later, it no longer deals in pigs and goats but has nevertheless become an important addition to the town of Kings Richington. The great and the good come here to shop most weekends and consider it fashionable and chic. They meet friends for posh coffee and a stroll around the square, telling each other that it's every bit as trendy as Notting Hill or Camden Town. But this approbation is soon to change — and in a shocking way.

CHAPTER ONE

The market stall that attracted much business, and invariably a long queue, was that of the Richington Ladies' Guild. Stocked with delicious homemade cakes, wine and preserves, it was nearly always sold out by lunchtime. The ladies of the Guild took it in turns to serve on a rota, which was drawn up by the president, Fenella Wilson — a homely, unremarkable lady, who put comfort before comeliness. Fenella earned a small income illustrating children's books, but it wasn't nearly enough for her to be self-sufficient. When she wasn't drawing woodland animals or waiting on her mother-in-law, Fenella provided the stall with her very popular homemade jams and chutneys.

On this significant Saturday in June, she was sharing both the stall and her woes with her close friend, Judith Kelly. Judith was a qualified car mechanic with her own garage on the Kings Richington bypass. As well as serving on the stall, her value to the Ladies' Guild was in logistics. She collected produce from members without transport and ferried them to the market.

Fenella was in full flow. 'I'm telling you, Jude, I've had just about enough of the old bag. Nothing I do is right. Her food is either too hot or too cold. I don't iron her blouses the way she likes, and today, she told me that her son could have done so much better than me and I should be grateful to have him.'

Judith frowned. 'Mothers-in-law are rarely the easiest people to get along with, but yours is a particularly spiteful old besom. What does David say?'

'Oh, Ida can do no wrong in his eyes. He's forty-two for goodness' sake, but to hear the way he talks to her, you'd think he was still five years old. His precious mummy is all he cares about. He just thinks I should try harder to please her.'

'Well, bugger that!' said Judith, vehemently. The genteel lady she was serving with a Victoria sponge looked shocked and hurried away with her cake, tutting. What kind of person was the Guild recruiting these days?

Fenella sighed. 'Last night, he was talking about making our house more comfortable for her. Apparently, she wants him to knock through her bedroom wall into my bedroom and convert it into a dressing room and en suite.'

'But you only have three bedrooms.'

'I know. That would mean I'd have to sleep with David again.'

'Fen, that's awful. You know how much you hated it.'

'I think the old cow suggested it on purpose, just to make my life more miserable than it already is.'

Judith squeezed her hand under the counter. 'You mustn't let her bully you.'

'I know, but what else can I do?'

'You could always leave David and come and live with me.'

Fenella squeezed her hand in return. 'I know and thank you — but I honestly don't see why I should be the one to leave. I grew up in that house. My mother left it to me, so that I'd always have a roof over my head. Illustrating is a pleasant enough job, but it doesn't make much money. I couldn't afford to live if I chucked David and his mother out, even if I was able to. I dare say they've got squatters' rights, or something.'

'How old is she? I don't suppose she's likely to snuff it, any time soon?'

'No such luck. She's only seventy-two. She keeps going on about her heart and how the doctor says her life hangs by a thread, but actually, she's as tough as old boots. She'll probably see us all out.' Fenella looked guilty. 'I have this recurring fantasy where I creep into her room at night and hold a pillow over her face.'

Judith shook her head. 'No, Fen, you mustn't do that. The police have sophisticated forensics these days. They could test the pillow for her saliva and your DNA.' She thought for a moment, chewing her lip. 'I'm sure I could come up with a smarter way of killing her.'

Fenella laughed, grimly. 'Well, you'd better think of one soon. The way I feel, I might just put my hands around her throat and squeeze, until she stopped squawking.'

'No, love, you mustn't do that, either. You'd leave marks on her neck. And there are things called "petechiae" — spots on the whites of her eyes that would show she'd been strangled.'

'You seem to know a lot about murder,' observed Fenella.

Judith shrugged. 'I read a lot of true crime. And I google stuff. You'd be surprised what you can learn on the internet. The challenge, of course, is not to get caught.'

* * *

When Fenella got home, Ida and David were looking at plans of the proposed new building work, spread out on the table.

'Oh, good, you're home at last, Fenella,' sniped Ida, not even looking at her. 'About time, too. I don't know what keeps you so long at that market stall. Gossiping, I imagine. Your husband wants his afternoon tea and so do I.'

Fenella bridled. 'Well, it wouldn't have hurt one of you to put the kettle on and butter a few scones. It isn't as if you're incapable, is it, Ida?'

'That's right! Expect an elderly lady to do your work for you. You always were lazy.' She turned to her son. 'You should have married that lovely girl who worked on the beauty counter in Boots. She had a pretty name — Sally, Sara, something like that. She was so fond of you. You'd have had a good, traditional marriage with a wife who recognized her duty. She would have looked after her mother-in-law without complaining.'

Fenella snapped. 'If you don't like it here, Ida, we could always get you a place at Laburnum Lodge. It's a very nice residential home and you know several of the ladies there. I'm sure you'd find it more congenial than living here with such incompetent service.'

Ida went puce. 'David, did you hear that? She wants to shut me away in a home.' She began sobbing, theatrically. 'With my weak heart, I'd be dead in a month. That's what you want, isn't it, you wicked woman? You want me dead.'

David scowled at Fenella and put his arms around his mother. 'It's all right, dear. Don't cry. Nobody's going to put you in a home. Fenella didn't mean it. She's just a bit tired, that's all.'

Later that evening, Ida declared herself far too upset to eat dinner. After two large glasses of sherry and much coaxing from David, she eventually managed to force down two pork chops, roast potatoes, carrots and peas, followed by a generous wedge of apple tart and custard. She then took herself off to bed with a dramatic headache and palpitations, brought on, she claimed, by Fenella's unpleasantness. She paused on the way out of the door, smirking nastily, as she delivered her Parthian shot. 'Of course, a *proper* daughter-in-law would have given me grandchildren.'

After Ida had gone, Fenella broached the subject of residential care again.

'Don't you think your mother would be happier at Laburnum Lodge? She already goes there to play bridge with some of the residents and it isn't as if she can't afford it.' Ida was well off, having sold her very large house and several acres of land, before moving in with them.

David lowered his newspaper. 'No, Fenella, I do not! No mother of mine is going to be bundled into a home, while I'm capable of looking after her.'

Fenella lost her temper. 'Yes, but that's just it, isn't it? You don't look after her — I do — and I'm fed up with it.'

'There's no need to screech at me. If you want me to help with Mother, I will, but really, it's a woman's job, don't you agree?' He went back to his newspaper, indicating that the discussion was at an end.

Fenella decided differently. 'Don't you think the time has come for you to tell her why she doesn't have grandchildren? Nor is she ever likely to.'

David threw down the newspaper. 'Please don't start that again, Fenella. We've had this conversation over and over and frankly, I'm sick of your insinuations.'

'But they aren't simply insinuations, are they, David? When I finally managed to get you to the specialist, he told us why I hadn't conceived. You're infertile. To put it bluntly, you're firing blanks — and you have been for the entire fifteen years of our marriage!'

David grimaced with distaste. 'Please, Fenella, don't use that coarse, market-traders' language here in our home. If I am "firing blanks," as you so vulgarly put it, it's through no fault of my own.'

'No,' Fenella retorted. 'It's your mother's fault! She's the one who wouldn't have you vaccinated as a child. Our specialist said it was orchitis from your mumps that had caused your sterility but it could have been treated if your mother had taken you to a doctor at the time. But she didn't, did she? She left you with your balls swollen up like big, red plums!'

He winced at the memory. 'Do you really want me to tell my mother that her neglect is the reason we can't have children? She'd be mortified. You must see that. I simply won't do it.'

'Of course you won't. You'd rather she kept sniping at me, inferring that I'm to blame, when you and I both know there's nothing wrong with me. And you wouldn't even discuss the possibility of a sperm donor.'

He coughed, embarrassed. 'If we used another man's sperm, the baby wouldn't be my child, nor Mother's grandchild, would it? It's better to leave things the way they are.'

'Not for me, it isn't! Well, the next time she has a pop at me about my abysmal failure to provide her with grandchildren, I'm going to tell her.'

David's face turned scarlet with temper and he seemed to be having trouble breathing. 'If you do that, Fenella, with Mother's heart the way it is, you may very well kill her — and I'd never forgive you.' He stood up and pulled a petulant face. 'I refuse to discuss this any longer. I'm going to bed.' He stomped off upstairs.

Fenella suspected he'd had tantrums like this as a toddler. She could imagine him lying on the floor, kicking his chubby little legs and holding his breath till he went blue and his mummy picked him up and cuddled him. Mothers, she conceded, had much to answer for, after their precious boys married and expected the same indulgences from their wives. She poured herself a large cognac and turned on the television. It was a murder mystery and despite the glib detective inspector and his chippy sergeant, the police were baffled. Fenella would never have considered herself capable of killing anyone, although she'd read somewhere that everyone is capable of at least one murder — it just needed sufficient provocation. She wondered, purely hypothetically, whether Jude would come up with a foolproof, totally infallible method of murdering Ida, without getting caught. And if she did, could she actually go through with it? Right at this moment, Fenella rather thought she could.

CHAPTER TWO

Detective Inspector Jack Dawes of the Metropolitan Murder Investigation Team examined the label on the wine bottle he'd just taken from the fridge. He held it out to his wife.

'Elderflower wine, Corrie? When did we start drinking this?'

Coriander Dawes was making crème brulée. She was trying it with a different kind of vanilla sugar before she incorporated it into the menu at Coriander's Cuisine, her catering company. 'I bought a few bottles from the Ladies' Guild's market stall. It's really good. Shut your eyes and taste some — it could almost be a Marlborough.'

Jack took a generous swig and swished it round his mouth. 'You're right. It's much better than I expected and very like a good Kiwi Sav.' He poured her a glass and took it over to where she was firing up her blowtorch to caramelize the sugar. It always made him nervous. 'Do you want me to do that?'

'No, thank you, darling. The last time I let you use my blowtorch, you set fire to the curtains.'

Jack pulled a face. 'It wasn't my fault. That torch bears a grudge.'

'I know. It's never forgiven you for dropping it on the patio after you used it to light the barbecue.' She pointed to the triangular dents in the handgrip. 'Look — it still has the scars, poor thing.'

Jack grinned and poured himself another glass of wine. He examined the label again. 'This stuff's thirteen per cent proof. Isn't that rather strong for homemade wine? I suppose the people on the stall have all the necessary licences and . . .'

Corrie sighed. 'Jack, have a day off, for goodness' sake. Nobody died. Just enjoy it.'

But DI Jack Dawes could no more 'have a day off' from being a copper than Corrie could forget to be a chef. It was what they were, rather than what they did. Their professions defined them and they were both very happy with the situation. They had married later in life, when each had already settled into a career and there were no dreary arguments over whose job took precedence or the amount of time they spent working.

'How come you're home so early, anyway?' Corrie asked. 'Usually the cleaners have to chuck you out around suppertime.'

Jack pinched an amuse-bouche from a tray where they were cooling and popped it in his mouth. It was still hot and he was unable to speak for a few moments. 'Not much on right now,' he mumbled.

Murder investigation teams investigated cases of murder, manslaughter, and attempted murder where the evidence of intent is unambiguous or where a risk assessment identifies substantial risk to life. There had been no such events on Jack's watch for a while — a couple of stabbings and some gang warfare but nothing that needed complex detective work. This was soon to change and in a rather spectacular fashion.

'I've got the team working on cold cases — murders that were never solved but are still open. Old George likes to give the public value for money even when things are quiet.' Chief Superintendent George Garwood was Jack's boss and keen on any results that might make him look good in the eyes of the commander, Sir Barnaby Featherstonehaugh. 'We've had the lads from Art Fraud in for the last couple of weeks. It seems there's a lot of it going on at the moment and they've traced some dodgy paintings to our area.'

'Really?' Corrie was surprised. 'I shouldn't have thought there were many fake Picassos and Dalís hanging on the walls of respectable Kings Richington folk.'

'Maybe not, but how can you tell what's fake and what's real? Turns out that sometimes, you can't. The Fraud boys reckon around twenty per cent of all the artworks in museums and galleries are fake — the market's rife with forged masterpieces.'

'All the same, I doubt whether the Kings Market is bristling with them. There's a stall outside the Coleville Gallery but they sell mostly antique bric-a-brac and collectibles. All the paintings are inside.' Corrie noticed another hors d'œuvre was missing from the tray. 'You'd better not eat too many of those. They're Carlene's latest experiment and she's very proud of them. She's coming to pick them up for the bistro later.'

Carlene was Corrie's deputy and the daughter she'd never had. She helped to run Corrie's Kitchen, a lucrative online and takeaway meals service, and together with her French boyfriend, Antoine, she had recently opened Chez Carlene, serving bistro food to younger customers. What had started with Corrie Dawes as a one-woman enterprise in a small industrial unit on the edge of town had grown into something of a culinary empire. It never ceased to amaze Corrie, who loved her job, how customers, especially the more affluent folk in Kings Richington, would prefer to pay someone else to cook their food. Coriander's Cuisine was in constant demand for dinner parties, functions and celebrations.

'I wonder how Bugsy is getting on,' said Corrie.

Jack's second-in-command, Detective Sergeant Michael 'Bugsy' Malone, was spending the weekend in Brighton with his fiancée, Iris. She had been widowed for some years and had never fancied travelling on her own. It was doubtful whether Bugsy had ever taken a holiday of any kind, having no one to share it with until now. Iris's husband had been a doctor, as was her son, Dr Daniel Griffin. Bugsy had saved Danny's life during a violent attack. Iris would be eternally grateful and the incident had made Bugsy a valued friend of the family.

'He'll be having a great time. Iris is very good for him.' Jack sneaked another amuse-bouche — a filo pastry cushion stuffed with something. He blew on it this time, but it didn't help. 'Dear God! What's inside this?'

Corrie glanced over her shoulder. 'Carlene calls those "Delhi Dreams." Bits of minced lamb with ginger, cayenne pepper and curry powder. They're very popular.'

Jack took a gulp of elderflower wine to put out the fire. 'Well, if people suddenly start dropping dead from food poisoning in Kings Richington, I'll know where to start looking.'

Jack may have been joking but both he and Corrie would be forced to take it seriously in the coming weeks.

CHAPTER THREE

On the following Friday afternoon, Ida Wilson returned from her bridge session at Laburnum Lodge just after five o'clock. She had gone out wearing an elaborate afternoon dress and jacket with court shoes and matching bag. The display of gold and diamond jewellery was to emphasize to the other ladies that she was financially superior and more refined. She put her head around the study door, where Fenella was drawing squirrels in party frocks. 'I'm going to lie down — I'm utterly exhausted. Wake me when it's time for my sherry.'

After a couple of hours, she swanned into the kitchen where Fenella was preparing the evening meal. She had changed into a fuchsia pink, feather-trimmed cape dress that Fenella knew had cost David the best part of a thousand pounds in Harvey Nichols. She'd seen it on his credit card statement.

'Isn't supper ready yet? I suppose it's too much to hope that you'll produce something halfway decent — goodness knows, it's taking you long enough. I don't know why David puts up with it. That pretty girl he was engaged to before you got your claws into him was a lovely little cook.'

Fenella had bought seabass that afternoon from Fred's fish stall at the market. It was always excellent quality and

13

very fresh and she was planning to serve it with a lemon and dill sauce.

Ida leaned over and poked at it with a fork. Her breath smelled strongly of sweet sherry, a partiality she'd picked up from the Laburnum Lodge bridge ladies. 'I don't want fish,' she announced, 'and I certainly shan't eat that muck. You got it cheap from the market, didn't you? Why couldn't you have bought a nice fillet of salmon or halibut? The amount of money I give David for my keep, I deserve something better than scraps off a stall.' She sat down on a kitchen chair and folded her arms. 'I fancy lasagne. Made from scratch, mind — none of that ready-meal rubbish from the supermarket that you hide in the freezer.'

Fenella went on preparing the fish without looking up. 'I'm sorry, Ida, but it's seabass or nothing. It's delicious and you'll enjoy it. I'm not making a separate meal just for you.'

'Oh, aren't you? We'll see about that!' Ida flounced off up to her room, fuming. She poured herself a stiff single malt from the bottle she kept hidden in her underwear drawer. She was too angry for sherry now and needed something stronger. Wait until David got back from the office. He'd soon put the cheeky cow in her place.

* * *

As soon as he came through the door, Ida came stomping downstairs and started complaining, before he'd even taken off his coat.

'David, you have to speak to Fenella. She's been really rude and nasty to me.'

David sighed. He was tired of constantly refereeing arguments between his wife and his mother. 'What is it this time, dear?'

'She's refusing to provide me with a decent, wholesome meal. At my age, and with my heart, I need proper nourishment, not a bit of old fish she bought off the market. Tell her, David. Make her cook me what I want.'

David went into the kitchen, with Ida close on his heels, keen to witness Fenella being torn off a strip. He went across to his wife and gave her his usual, perfunctory peck on the cheek. David Wilson was a beige sort of man — lacklustre hair, sallow complexion and dreary manner.

Fenella was peeling asparagus spears. 'Good evening, David, and before you say anything, we're all having seabass for supper.'

He turned to Ida. 'Well, that sounds very nice, Mother — light and easy to digest.'

Ida scowled. Things weren't going the way she wanted. 'I'm allergic to fish. I daren't touch it.'

Fenella laughed at her. 'No, you're not. I've seen you put away a plateful of cod and chips that would challenge a burly bricklayer, never mind an elderly lady — with no ill effects at all. And what about all the sardines and seafood paella you ate on our holiday in Spain?'

'That was different. They were properly cooked by people who knew what they were doing.' She besought her son. 'Do you want to have to call an ambulance in the night, when my throat swells up and I can't breathe?'

'No, of course not, dear. What would you like instead of fish?'

'I've already told her. I want lasagne but she refuses to cook it for me.'

Wearily, David appealed to Fenella. 'That doesn't sound unreasonable to me, darling. Surely it wouldn't take long to make Mother a simple lasagne, if that's what she fancies?'

Fenella flung down her paring knife. It was too much. Ida had gone too far, whining to her precious son so he would take her side. Well, this time, she wasn't going to get away with it.

'If it's so simple, then she can make it herself — and you can eat it with her. I'm going out!' She grabbed her handbag and a coat from the hall and went out, slamming the door behind her.

By the time she had driven into town, she had calmed down a little. She parked in the high street, took out her phone and speed-dialled Judith.

'Hello, Jude. It's me, Fen.'

'Yes, I know it's you. Your pic comes up on my phone when you ring. Are you OK?' With the phone cradled against her shoulder, Judith grabbed a rag and wiped the worst of the engine oil from her hands.

'No, not really.' Fenella recounted the bitter altercation. 'I felt like picking up the wet fish and slapping her round the face with it.'

Judith laughed. 'Never mind, love. I'll have finished working on this car in ten minutes. Let's eat out somewhere, then pick up a couple of bottles of wine and take them back to my flat. You won't be able to drive home afterwards, so you'll have to stay the night.'

'Lovely. Just what I need. Where shall we meet?'

'How about that new bistro — Chez Carlene? I've heard the food is excellent.'

'OK, I'll meet you outside. We'll choose lots of expensive dishes and I'll pay with David's credit card.'

It was while they were sitting inside the bistro, trying to decide what to order, that Judith spotted the car. Being a mechanic, cars were her stock-in-trade. She nudged Fenella, who was torn between cassoulet and smoked duck breast. 'Fen, isn't that David's Lexus?' she pointed to the car that had just pulled up across the road.

Fenella looked. It was indeed the expensive saloon that Ida had bought for her son as a birthday present. 'Well, I wonder what he's doing here? You don't think he followed me, do you?'

But David Wilson was clearly oblivious to the two women, sitting in the window of the bistro on the corner. He climbed out of the car, went around to open the passenger door and helped someone out. Fenella recognized the flutter of fuchsia feathers. Ida was dolled up to the nines and laughing merrily. He offered her his arm and together they went into Le Canard Bleu, the most expensive restaurant in Kings Richington. It was owned, together with several more establishments, by a wealthy French family. Antoine, their son, was Carlene's boyfriend and the inspiration behind Chez Carlene.

'Well, would you believe it?' Fenella exploded. 'He's taking the old witch out to dinner! I can't remember the last time he took me out for a meal. What a bloody cheek!'

* * *

Fenella set out the Ladies' Guild stall half an hour early on Saturday morning. She'd spent a happy and relaxed Friday night at Judith's flat and she had no intention of going home to face interrogation about why she'd seen fit to spend the night with a friend. Instead, she'd driven straight to the market. Last night, she had ignored the calls and messages from David asking when she was coming home to make Ida's cocoa and get her ready for bed. In his usual pompous fashion, he'd expressed the fervent hope that she didn't expect *him* to do it. It simply wouldn't be appropriate and Ida was very tired. He knew, he said, that Fenella would eventually see sense, stop being selfish and do her duty. *Well, good luck with that!* thought Fenella. *Of course the old bitch was tired — she was full of food and wine from her posh dinner at Le Canard Bleu. She could put herself to bed!*

The market always lifted Fenella's spirits. It was the cheery hustle and bustle as much as anything. Other traders were setting out their goods and calling 'Good morning' to her as she arranged jars of jam, marmalade and chutney in tempting towers along the counter. The cakes, pies and other fresh produce would come later when the ladies of the Guild brought them to her. Market-goers were already filling their shopping bags with fruit and vegetables and selecting bunches of summer flowers from the fragrant florist's stall.

Rhythmic reggae music pulsated from Jericho's Music, a stall at the lower end of the street. It was managed — if you could call it that — by an elderly Rastafarian with a particular liking for Bob Marley and sweet Jamaican rum, which he drank most of the day. A few of the locals had complained about the noise but Fenella liked it. It prompted dreams of blissful Caribbean islands and warm sunshine.

Jericho was a striking character in baggy shirt and trousers with a colourful, knitted hat over his dreadlocks. As well as music, he sold tee-shirts, scarves and posters printed with reggae artists and pictures of Jamaican beaches with white sand and cobalt sea. Over the years, he had become a well-loved icon of the market, popular with stallholders and shoppers alike. Fenella and Judith had romanticised about a Caribbean cruise together, more in hope than expectation. Fenella couldn't see it ever happening — not with David and his ghastly mother in her life, making constant demands.

* * *

Later that morning, after she'd serviced Chief Superintendent Garwood's car, Judith arrived at the Ladies' Guild stall carrying two posh coffees and a large box of apple pies. The pies had been cooked by an elderly neighbour who could no longer get to the market but still liked to contribute. Judith plonked the box down in front of Fenella and handed her a coffee.

'Ethylene glycol!' she announced, without preamble.

'And a very good morning to you, too.' Fenella laughed, pleased to see her as always. 'And there I was, thinking it was a skinny latte.'

'No, listen, Fen. I've been working this out all morning. I believe it's the answer to your mother-in-law problem. The idea came to me while I was servicing old George Garwood's Audi. Ethylene glycol. That's antifreeze to you. I've got gallons of it back at the garage. It's the really strong stuff and highly toxic.'

'What are you suggesting — that we drown her in it?'

'No, that we poison her with it.'

Fenella looked at Jude's face. 'Bloody hell, Jude. You're serious, aren't you?'

'Deadly serious, pardon the pun. It's sweet-tasting, so if you put it in her tea, for example, she won't have a clue that anything's wrong and it works fast.'

'But won't it look suspicious when she starts frothing at the mouth or something?'

Jude shook her head. 'Didn't you say that Ida likes a drink?

'Yes, she puts away a fair amount of whisky and sherry.'

'Perfect. The initial symptoms of antifreeze poisoning look like the results of too much alcohol — slurred speech, staggering about and confusion. After that, the person's heart rate goes up and they hyperventilate, so they appear to have died of a heart attack. You said Ida was under the doctor with her heart, so he'd simply sign the death certificate with no need of a post-mortem. I'm telling you, Fen, ethylene glycol is the number one homicide poison in the United States. For the modern killer, antifreeze has a lot of advantages over Victorian arsenic. For a start, there's nothing suspicious about having it around, especially in a garage.'

Fenella thought about it. 'We couldn't put it in her tea. She doesn't take sugar and she wouldn't drink it if it was sweet. What about chocolates? She eats boxfuls at a time. David is always buying them for her.'

Judith shook her head. 'No, too fiddly, and we'd have to do all of them to make sure she got enough of the stuff to be fatal.'

A customer interrupted them, wanting two jars of strawberry jam. After she'd served her, Fenella said, 'Ida likes jam, though. I've known her get through a whole pot at breakfast. Could we put it in jam?'

'Absolutely. Several dollops on her toast and it's, "Goodnight, Ida, you evil old bat."'

'Do you know how much to give her? We don't want her just to feel a bit ill — I'd be the one who ended up nursing her.'

Judith pursed her lips. 'That's the tricky bit. According to the experts, and I quote, "It's difficult to quantify the amounts that were consumed by people who have succumbed to the toxic effects. This leads to uncertainty around what is the human lethal dose." It's generally considered that a fatal dose can be as little as a fluid ounce — about what you'd get in a shot glass. But a lot depends on the weight, age and general health of the victim.'

'Blimey, you've really done your research, haven't you? What does all that mean?' asked Fenella.

'It means we need to practise on someone about the same age and weight as Ida, before we go in for the kill.'

CHAPTER FOUR

Across the street, in the coolly elegant Coleville Gallery,
Sasha de Coleville was selecting suitable items for her stall
— eponymously named, Sasha's Souvenirs. It made very little profit but proved useful as an incentive to entice people
into the gallery. Her husband, Ludovic, handled the important works, having a Master's degree in Art History and a
smart business sense. He was witty, well-dressed and handsome — an accomplished charmer who invariably got what
he wanted.

Sasha dealt with the popular collectibles. She was beautiful in an obvious kind of way, with long, honey-blonde
hair, an enviable, if somewhat lean, figure and a vacuous
personality. They were viewed by the staid locals as Kings
Richington's answer to the Kardashians, a glamorous, glitzy
couple with an extravagant lifestyle.

Sasha picked up two porcelain figurines — a girl carrying flowers in her apron and a boy with a basket of fruit.
'Ludo, what do you think these are worth?'

He glanced at them. 'Whatever you can get, babe.
They're truly hideous.' He carried on carefully positioning
a painting of a nude by a local artist where it could be seen
immediately on entering the gallery. He stood back to admire

it, then adjusted the lighting. 'Will you be OK on your own, today, Sash? I have to go into the city for meetings with some suppliers.'

'I suppose so. What do I do if someone wants to buy one of the paintings?'

'They all have the price on them, my sweet. Just don't let them haggle.'

'What about those rather nice ones, down in the cellar? They don't have prices on them.'

Ludovic's expression changed. 'Don't sell any of those. If anyone comes in enquiring about a particular painting, take their name and contact details and tell them I'll get back to them.'

'OK. Whatever you say. Will you be back for supper?'

'Probably not. Go ahead without me.'

Don't worry, I intend to, thought Sasha. She had plans for a meeting of her own.

* * *

An hour later, Ludovic de Coleville emerged from the London underground at Aldgate East tube station and hailed a black cab.

'Where to, guv'nor?'

Ludovic consulted his mobile where he'd noted the address. 'Flat 23b, Downside Road, please.'

The taxi driver clocked the impeccable three-piece suit and handmade shoes. 'You sure, mate? That manor's a bit — you know — dodgy. Shouldn't want you to get mugged nor nuffink.'

'I'll be fine, thank you, driver.'

'D'you want me to put your bag in the boot?'

Ludovic held the expensive, black Italian leather holdall close to him. 'No, thank you. It'll be fine here in the back with me.'

The taxi pulled up outside number 23a. It was a run-down kebab shop in what would be described by pejorative social analysts as one of the more deprived areas of London. Ludovic could see what the driver meant by 'dodgy.' He got out and paid the man.

'That's 23b, guv'nor — up there.' The driver pointed to a window above the shop with a grubby curtain across it. 'The door's round the side.'

The door, with dark green paint peeling off it, opened directly onto a flight of dingy stairs. Ludovic climbed warily, watching where he put his feet. Every stair creaked ominously as if it could give way at any minute. At the top was a hand-written sign with an arrow pointing across the landing. *Vince Parker — Private Investigator.* Even as he pushed the door open, Ludovic wondered if he'd made the right choice. A business colleague had recommended this man, having hired him for some not-entirely-legal investigation work and apparently, with excellent results.

Vince Parker sat behind a mock-mahogany desk which — Ludovic noted with distaste — was made from cheap fibreboard. It was cluttered with papers, dirty mugs and a half-eaten cheese roll. Parker stood up and held out a hand.

'Mr de Coleville? Please take a seat and tell me how I can help you.'

Ludovic looked at the grimy chair that had no doubt accommodated the backsides of umpteen desperate blokes and for the second time, he wondered if he'd made the right choice. There were private investigators much closer to home that he might have used but he couldn't risk being spotted going into one. For that reason, and more importantly, because he didn't want anyone who knew him looking too closely into his affairs, Ludovic had chosen Vince Parker. The man certainly looked like the stereotypical idea of a seedy private eye — faded jeans, a jacket that had once been part of a suit and a greasy, greying ponytail. *At least he won't stand out in a crowd*, thought Ludovic. He began, tentatively.

'It's my wife, Mr Parker. I think she's having an affair.'

'Please, call me Vince. I take it you want to know who the man is and you need some photographs of them together?'

'Yes, that's pretty much it. Can you do that?'

'Meat and drink to me, Mr de Coleville. The Parker Investigation Bureau provides discreet and confidential services using a wide range of observational and research techniques to gather intelligence and achieve the results clients want.'

It was clear, thought Ludovic, *that he'd learned his mission statement off by heart and trotted it out to every client.* 'Do you have a licence, Vince? I don't see any certificates on your walls.'

'The private investigation sector isn't currently regulated in the UK and unfortunately, contains its share of rogue operators. I can assure you I am not one of them, Mr de Coleville. My charges are forty pounds an hour, plus expenses. When would you like me to start?'

'Straight away, please. I've written all the details in here.' He opened his holdall and handed over a file with a photograph of Sasha, mobile numbers and other relevant information.

Vince glanced at it. 'May I ask — what led you to suspect that your wife was being unfaithful?'

Ludovic gave it some thought. 'Well, the usual things, I suppose. She doesn't answer her phone if I'm in the room, she's careful I don't see any messages on it, she gets irritated if I question her about where she's going and she wears more make-up when she goes out alone.'

'Do you have any idea who the man is? I take it, it is a man.'

'Oh yes, it's a man all right, but I haven't a clue who he is.'

That, really, was the crux of the problem. It was a matter of supreme indifference to Ludovic that his wife was seeing someone else — he had already decided she would soon be his ex-wife — but he suspected that the man might be motivated by something other than lust. Sasha wasn't smart enough to know if she was being manipulated and he couldn't afford to allow anyone to upset what was an extremely lucrative enterprise. Sasha knew a little, but not all, of his business affairs. If she let slip something incriminating to her lover, it could have very unpleasant repercussions.

Vince stood up. 'Leave it to me, Mr de Coleville. I'll contact you as soon as I have any information. Once we know who the man is, the action you take will be up to you. Unless, of course, you want me to hand him over to some discouragement operatives. I have a few contacts in that line of business.'

Ludovic was horrified. 'No, no — nothing like that. I just want to know who he is. I'll deal with it after that.' He knew from his colleague that Vince Parker had done time for various misdemeanours including grievous bodily harm. He wanted nothing to do with any violence. Not unless it became absolutely necessary. 'I'll wait to hear from you.'

* * *

After leaving Vince Parker, Ludovic hailed another taxi and made for the Barbican Centre. Instead of loitering in the labyrinthine arts complex, tempting though it was, Ludovic had more serious business to attend to. He headed to a lesser-known gallery, off the main drag but within walking distance.

With the accent very firmly on conceptualism, the window of the Slater Art Gallery displayed a replica of Marcel Duchamp's *Fountain* — a porcelain urinal. Ludovic shook his head, wondering whether he was in the right business. He hadn't yet shaken off the grubby feeling that had persisted, even after he'd left Vince Parker's office. The urinal in the gallery window hadn't helped. But once inside, the calming decor and soft music restored his equilibrium. The chimes, on opening the door, alerted the receptionist, a smart young lady in a navy suit and crisp, white blouse.

He treated her to his dazzling smile. 'Good afternoon, Monica.'

'Mr de Coleville, how nice to see you again. Mr Slater is expecting you.' She led the way through the gallery to a room at the back. Rob Slater, unlike Vince Parker, was seated behind a genuine mahogany desk — immaculate and burnished.

'Drink, Ludo? Or are you driving?'

'No, I came in a taxi. Whisky, please. A large one. I need it after doing business with your private eye. I felt I needed a shower after I came out.'

Slater laughed. 'Yes, he is pretty grim, but effective and discreet. I can't over-emphasize how important it is that your end of the business stays confidential. How much does your wife know about our transactions?'

'Not much. Only enough to enable her to deal with the packing and dispatching. But the little she does know could be problematic, if she's careless enough to blab it to someone smart who might get curious.'

'If that happens, you might have to get Vince to deal with it.'

Ludovic grimaced. 'I guess the end justifies the means.'

Slater refilled their glasses. 'What have you got for me?'

Ludovic opened the leather holdall. 'A Picasso drawing and a small bronze stick figurine by Brancusi. Both are excellent examples, I'm sure you'll agree.'

Slater was impressed. 'Very nice, Ludo. These will finance an enterprise I'm running with an import–export company. What about the larger paintings you promised me?'

'They should be with you next week when my transport driver is available. I can't trust just any old logistics company. They ask too many questions.'

'Where are you storing them in the meantime?'

'In a vault built into the cellar of the Coleville Gallery. They should be safe there.'

'I hope so. If anyone pokes about and finds them, it could go badly for you, Ludo.'

'I know. That's why I need to know who Sasha is seeing. Trust me. I have it under control.'

'Money in your offshore account as usual?'

'Yes, that'll be fine.'

CHAPTER FIVE

Detective Inspector Aakash — 'Call me Ash' — Banerjee, was sitting at the front of the incident room, sharing intelligence with members of the Murder Investigation Team. As head of the Met's Arts and Antiques Fraud Unit, the Detective Inspector had come to Kings Richington, hoping to track down some forgeries, which he believed had found their way into the area.

'We don't have exact information, but we know art crime is extensive and becoming more and more prolific, particularly where it's hidden away somewhere in the suburbs.'

DC Aled Williams, grateful to have a diversion from pursuing the murderers of long-dead victims, was unconvinced. 'Does that mean that there may be a fake Jackson Pollock hanging in a junk shop somewhere, but nobody's noticed?'

Ash laughed. 'I doubt if the works of Jackson Pollock would go unnoticed, given that his style was to put a large canvas on the floor and walk around it, chucking on various kinds of paint.'

'Surely that wouldn't be too difficult to forge,' observed Jack.

'You're absolutely right. Pollock fakes are still cropping up in all sorts of places. He's one of the most-forged post war artists. In 2007, one of his "silver drip" paintings sold for seventeen million dollars. Four years later, it was found to contain yellow paint pigments not commercially available until 1970. Pollock died in 1956.'

Detective Sergeant Malone finished his bacon roll and wiped his greasy fingers on a paper napkin instead of down his trousers, like he usually did. This was one of several habits that had changed since his engagement to Iris.

'Sounds to me like this Pollock bloke made shedloads of dosh out of crackpots who were afraid to criticize his "art" because everyone else reckoned it was good — like the emperor's new clothes. Even I could chuck some paint about and pretend it was a masterpiece.'

Ash grinned. 'If you're planning to imitate Jack the Dripper, Bugsy, you've already made a start. You've dropped tomato ketchup down your tie.'

'Is art fraud really so important in the greater scheme of things, sir?' asked DC Gemma Fox. 'The job of the Murder Investigation Team is to stop folk killing each other and arrest them if they do. That seems to take priority, in my opinion.' It was the reason Gemma had been so keen to join the team.

'You're right, Gemma,' said Ash. 'And if it was just a case of some rich collector getting ripped off by illegally buying what he thinks is a stolen Matisse that turns out to be a fake, I'd agree. You could argue that it's just criminals scamming other criminals. But the end game is to break up the organized-crime gangs. The money obtained from the sale of forgeries is funding serious crimes around the world — drugs, firearms, trafficking, money laundering and other nasty activities. If you know where to look, there are signs of it all around.'

'Yes, but organized-crime gangs don't affect us much in the UK, surely?' said Aled.

'On the contrary, every year, we unwittingly drink millions of bottles of untaxed Italian wine, smuggled in by the Calabrian mafia. The illegal waste-disposal industry is worth billions. And if you get your car washed by hand, at a pop-up garage in a car park, chances are you're being served by someone who has been trafficked. Don't even get me started on slavery. Britain is said to host over seven thousand different organized-crime groups costing the country 100 million pounds a day in crime and lost revenue. Big cities have become hotbeds of international criminals, from cocaine kings and street gangsters to villains who specialize in robberies and contract killings. These new forms of crime defy the old stereotypes.'

'Some days, I feel like an old stereotype,' Bugsy complained glumly.

'Nonsense, Sarge,' said Gemma. 'We rookies learn stuff from you every day.'

'Believe it or not,' continued Ash, 'there are more crime syndicates than there are staff members in the National Crime Agency tasked with smashing them. I'd say that was pretty serious, wouldn't you?'

'Where do you want to start, Ash?' asked Jack.

'Before I deploy a full team on this, I thought I'd just turn over a few stones and see if anything crawls out. You have to be unobtrusive in my line of policing until you're certain you've got something. These crooks can vanish into thin air before you can grab them. I won't get under the feet of your lads, Jack, but some help with local turf and known criminals would be useful.'

Jack nodded. 'It's pretty quiet at the moment so feel free to pick our brains. DC "Mitch" Mitchell and Sergeant Norman Parsloe from uniform have a wealth of local knowledge. Norman knows all the resident villains — he's nicked most of them. He may be able to fill in some background information.'

'Thanks, guys. I'll stay in touch.'

* * *

While DI Dawes and his team were learning about the murky world of art fraud and the organized-crime gangs that feed off it, Sasha de Coleville was learning about the murky world of adultery, in a bedroom in the Richington Arms Hotel.

'Are you sure nobody recognized us when we checked in, darling?'

David Wilson held her closer and whispered in her ear. 'Of course not, sweetheart. Why would anyone recognize us right out here on the edge of town? It isn't as though either of us would spend time here normally.'

She sat up and ran her fingers through her long, blonde hair. 'No, I suppose not. It's just that there was a scruffy-looking man downstairs in the bar when we came in. I thought he was watching us. He seemed to take notice when you ordered champagne to be brought up to the room.'

'That's only because the kind of people who come here don't drink champagne. I was surprised they even had any. As it is, they haven't chilled it properly. Next time, we'll spend a weekend somewhere in the country, away from Kings Richington.'

'There's going to be a next time, then?'

'Of course there is,' assured David. 'You want us to go on seeing each other, don't you?'

'I've wanted to be with you ever since we were first engaged. I was heartbroken when you ended it. I just drifted into marriage with Ludovic by default.'

'I should have married you. Fenella was a mistake, always making demands and arguing with Mother. It's like a battle-field at home some days, and I'm in the middle, trying to keep the peace.'

'Poor you.' Sasha put her arms around him. 'It isn't as if you have children to ease the pressure. Why did you never have any? I've often wondered.'

David avoided her gaze. 'Oh, I always wanted them, but Fenella refused. Something about not wanting to deal with dirty nappies and baby sick.'

'Ludo never had time for children, either. He's too busy making money. I know we have a lovely home on the river and the gallery and everything, but there has to be more to marriage than that, doesn't there?'

'Of course there does, my angel. Once I'm free of Fenella and you've left Ludovic, we'll be together like we should have been all those years ago. You, me and Mother. She was always so fond of you. Now come here and show me how much you want me.'

Sasha held back. 'What if I get pregnant, David? I'm still young. Would you mind?'

David shrugged. 'No, I wouldn't mind. But don't let's worry about that now. Everything will be fine — I promise.'

Two hours later, when they checked out, Sasha noticed that the scruffy man with the greasy grey ponytail was still in the bar. What she didn't notice was that he took several photographs of them with his hidden camera.

CHAPTER SIX

The flat above Judith's garage, Kelly's Car Services and Repairs, was cosy, if somewhat minimalist. Judith had little time for what she called 'knick-knackery.' For Fenella, it was a safe haven from the hostilities at home. That evening, David had gone out — she didn't know where — so she had left Ida watching a quiz programme on television and driven to the flat. Now she was in Judith's tiny kitchen, cooking spaghetti Bolognese.

'You didn't need to cook for us, Fen.' Judith was opening a bottle of Montepulciano d'Abruzzo to go with the pasta. 'We could have gone to Chez Carlene again.'

Fenella pushed a strand of damp hair behind her ear. 'I like cooking for us and I know you don't eat properly. You're working in the garage all day, so it's no wonder you don't feel like cooking in the evening. At least you appreciate my food and don't accuse me of trying to poison you.'

'I take it Ida is still being a bitch?'

'She doesn't know how to be anything else. David's always out somewhere on business, so I have to manage her on my own. Tonight, as soon as her precious son had left the house, she started on me — I don't take enough care of my appearance, I'm not loving enough to my husband, my housework is slovenly and it's such a shame her dear David is stuck with someone who doesn't know how to be a proper wife. Honestly, Jude, if I hadn't gone out, I'd have taken a brick to her.'

Judith handed her a glass of wine. 'You mustn't do anything hasty, Fen. I've been thinking. Who do we know who is around Ida's age, about the same weight and would be a good subject to try out the ethylene glycol? It needs to be someone who isn't too close to us, so we aren't obvious suspects.'

Fenella stopped stirring the sauce and gave it some thought. 'Someone on the market would be good. There are lots of traders but none of them is directly linked to us.'

'That's what I thought. And it shouldn't be too difficult if we do it on a Saturday, when the market is crowded.'

'But we're not actually going to kill someone, are we?' Fenella was anxious.

'No, course not. Not yet, anyway. We'll administer a trial amount, just enough to have a slight effect, and we'll watch how long it takes to work. That will enable us to calculate the correct dosage to put an end to Ida.'

They considered the stallholders, one by one, while they ate.

'Fred the fishmonger?' suggested Fenella.

'No, he's too skinny,' said Jude. 'How much do you reckon Ida weighs?'

'At least twelve stone. She puts away as much food as David and me put together, despite having what she calls a "delicate constitution". And it's all heavy stuff, full of carbs. She won't even touch salad — claims she can't swallow lettuce.'

'What about Beryl? She's the one with the vintage clothing stall, all fringes, beads and shawls. Who wears that stuff, anyway?' Judith's wardrobe consisted of trousers, shirts and overalls — mostly overalls. She had one posh frock which hadn't seen the light of day since her nephew's christening and he'd just started at university.

'No, not Beryl. She's diabetic. She wouldn't touch anything sweet.'

One by one, they considered each stall-owner as a potential guinea-pig, starting at the high end, with Sasha de Coleville's collectibles, down to the lower end, which was Jericho's music stall.

'That's it,' said Judith, suddenly. 'What about old Jericho? He's the right age and weight and spends most of his time asleep inside his stall. It's more of a shack than a stall. I believe he spends the night in there after the market closes, rather than going home. Maybe he doesn't even have a home.'

'It's the sweet, treacly Jamaican rum he drinks. They make it from molasses and cane sugar,' said Fenella. 'You can even smell it when you walk past.'

'What you can smell, Fen, is *ganja*.' Fenella looked blank. 'Jamaican Jive? Wacky Weed?' Judith laughed. 'Fen, you're such an innocent. It's marijuana you can smell.'

'Oh, I didn't realize.' The penny finally dropped. 'What with that and the rum, it's no wonder Jericho is so cheerful all the time. I wonder why he's called Jericho. It isn't a typically Rastafarian name, is it?'

'I'm told his Jamaican mum was a very Christian lady. Anyway, he's perfect for our experiment. One of us will nip down to his stall when he goes to that global street food place for his lunch. We'll slip the antifreeze in his rum bottle. He always has jerk chicken so I doubt he'll notice any difference in the taste.'

Fenella was still anxious. 'It won't harm him, will it? Not permanently? He's a lovely old bloke and I wouldn't want to make him seriously ill.'

'No,' assured Judith. 'He won't feel much worse than the hangovers he has most mornings. Leave it to me. I'll just give him a tiny amount. I've got a plunger thingy to measure the dose. Then we'll watch and see how long it takes to work.'

* * *

On Saturday afternoon, Corrie Dawes was buying venison from Good Game, the butcher who had a stall in the market. A client was planning a dinner party and had asked Coriander's Cuisine for Venison Wellington as the main course. Corrie bought a lot of meat from this supplier — the quality was exceptional and met her very high standards. She was watching Mary, the master butcher, skilfully trim the venison fillet, when a commotion down at the far end of the street caught her attention. Jericho was staggering about among the shoppers, pushing people aside and shouting. Corrie knew he was drunk fairly often and the police turned a blind eye to his marijuana habit, but he wasn't known for being disorderly. He was clutching at his chest and eventually, he collapsed in the road. A small crowd began to gather around him.

'Jericho must have started drinking early,' said Mary. She wrapped the venison. 'I've never seen him pass out at this time of day. I hope he's OK.'

Neighbouring stallholders helped him up and carried him back to the battered armchair by his stall. It was his habit to sit there, when he wasn't dancing in the street to the reggae music he played from his stand. Someone must have called an ambulance, because shoppers stood back to allow it through. Shortly after, Corrie saw the paramedics stretcher Jericho into the back and drive off with siren and lights.

Further down the market, hidden behind the piles of cakes and pies on the Ladies' Guild stall, Fenella and Judith had been watching — first with interest and then with alarm.

'Blimey,' said Judith, 'That wasn't supposed to happen. He was only meant to have mild symptoms. Just a bit drunk and confused, that's all.'

'Did you give him too much of the stuff?' asked Fenella. She watched the ambulance disappear in the direction of Kings Richington Infirmary.

Judith shook her head vigorously. 'No, I don't think so. I measured the dose, like we agreed. Trouble is, there's so much uncertainty about how much antifreeze will actually kill someone and what percentage of it is ethylene glycol.'

'Well, I think we'll need to increase the dose for Ida. I don't want her stumbling about the house, squawking, before she snuffs it.'

* * *

It was Jack Dawes's day off but Chief Superintendent Garwood had called him to the station to discuss the monthly report and clear-up figures. It seemed that the Murder Investigation Team was not solving cold cases as fast as he'd have liked. As Jack had pointed out, many of them dated back several years and in some cases, the police hadn't even found a body. Not much to go on. Garwood had simply insisted that they look harder.

'What have you been up to, Norman?' asked Bugsy, to break the monotony.

'Uniform got a call from the council, asking if someone would take a look at Jericho's old shack. They wanted it made secure because all his stuff's still in it,' replied Sergeant Parsloe. 'I went out in the area car. Turned out we needn't have bothered. His grandson, Desmond, was already there, fixing a padlock to the door. I don't think that young man likes the police.'

'What makes you think that, Sarge?' asked Gemma.

'Well, he seemed really suspicious of why I was there. So I asked him straight out, didn't I? It never hurts for the police to try and gain trust in the community. I said, "What is it you don't like about police officers, son?" He replied . . .' Norman pulled out his notebook, where he'd tried to write down exactly what Desmond had said, just how he'd said it. He showed Gemma.

She grinned. 'Are you sure that's what he said, Sarge? That he can't smoke his weed in peace? Did he use those words . . . or is that just your spelling?'

'Yes, DC Fox, I wrote it down phonetically, before you start accusing me of something unpleasant. That's exactly what he said.'

She giggled. 'Desmond and I were at uni together. He has a first-class honours degree in Politics and Philosophy and speaks with a cut-glass accent. We used to tease him about it. He's standing as Tory MP at the next bi-election. I think he was pulling your leg, Sarge.'

Norman grunted. 'Well, that's as may be. I can take a joke as well as the next copper. Anyway, I asked if he would fetch his granddad's stuff when convenient, in case it gets nicked.'

* * *

By the time he got home, Jack was ready for a cold beer, rugby on the television and no more talk of corpses. He put his head out of the back door where Corrie and Carlene were loading up the van to take to Coriander's Cuisine industrial unit.

'I was in the market buying ingredients this afternoon,' Corrie said. 'Poor old Jericho collapsed and they took him to hospital in an ambulance.'

Not more *corpses*, thought Jack. 'Is he OK?'

'No, he carked it,' said Carlene, shortly. 'Dicky ticker, they reckon. He didn't do himself any favours, did he? Booze and bad baccy for most of his life. Shame though. He brought sunshine to the market, even when it rained. People will miss him and his blasts of Bob Marley.'

Corrie agreed. 'Iris said that Dan had warned him several times about his lifestyle but he took no notice.'

'Iris is Sergeant Bugsy's fiancée, isn't she?' said Carlene. Bugsy had been something of a father figure to her during her formative years at Coriander's Cuisine and she was very fond of him.

'That's right, and Dan is Dr Griffin, her son.'

'Can I go and drink this beer before it gets warm, please?' begged Jack.

'Of course you can, sweetheart. Carlene and I are going to be busy at the Cuisine until late. I've left you cold game pie with quince and cranberry jelly in the fridge.' She reached up on tiptoe but still only managed to kiss him on the chin.

CHAPTER SEVEN

Ludovic de Coleville had gone out briefly to liaise with his private eye. Vince Parker had phoned to say that he had some news for him. Reluctantly, he'd left Sasha in charge of the gallery.

They'd arranged to meet in an unobtrusive teashop down at the lower end of the high street. Parker had arrived first and ordered tea. It was very strong and came in thick, white mugs.

Ludovic pushed his to one side with distaste. 'What do you have for me?'

'I've found your wife's lover. This file contains my full report with photographs of them together in a hotel. I imagine this is all you need. My bill is in there too.'

Ludovic opened the file, curious to see who would be dim-witted enough to want to spend time in a hotel room, in the middle of the day, with Sasha.

'As you can see, Mr de Coleville, the man's name is David Wilson. He works for a retail company in the city and lives with his wife and mother in Kings Richington.'

'Well, well — David "Weedy" Wilson,' said Ludovic. 'We were at school together. He's one of my wife's old flames. They were engaged, I believe, but he broke it off. The only surprising thing is that he should come crawling back for more, when he had successfully got shot of her. Thank you, Mr Parker, I have all I need.' He took out his cheque book.

'Er — I prefer cash, Mr de Coleville. I find in my profession that cheques aren't always reliable and attract unwelcome interest from the tax inspector.'

Ludovic shrugged. What a grubby little man. He felt contaminated, just being in the same café with him. 'I don't carry that sort of cash around on me. Come to the gallery tomorrow afternoon and I'll have it ready for you.'

* * *

Detective Inspector Banerjee had drawn something of a blank in his quest for seeking out the alleged forgeries. He had investigated the main galleries in the area with no success. Most gallery owners had expressed their disapproval that the police should even consider they would handle anything illegal. One or two had been outraged at the very idea. Ash decided that it might be more fruitful if he looked at the smaller businesses and eventually he found himself outside the Coleville Gallery.

'Good morning.' Ash held out his warrant card. 'Mrs de Coleville? I'm doing a survey for the Metropolitan Police Arts and Antiques Fraud Unit. I wonder if I might take a look around.'

Sasha examined the card. 'Certainly, Detective Inspector. Help yourself. May I ask what it is you're looking for?'

'Oh, nothing specific, madam. Just a routine inspection.'

'My husband is the art expert. He's just popped out but he should be back shortly. Can I get you something while you're waiting? A coffee, maybe?'

'Thank you, that would be very nice.' Ash decided he'd drawn another blank. If this lady knew anything about forgeries, she wasn't showing any furtive signs of guilt. He did a cursory tour of the gallery, which was bigger and loftier than it looked from outside. It was a Grade II listed building, built around 1810, according to the brochure that Sasha had given him. It reached up over two floors, each with a galleried landing and ornate, carved balustrades. The paintings occupied the ground floor, ceramics on the second and sculptures at the top. Ash searched for any telltale signs but found none. Sasha returned with the coffee.

He sipped it. 'Is this all your stock, or do you have any other artwork stored somewhere?'

Sasha wondered what she should do. Ludo had said that if anyone asked about any 'special' paintings, she should take their contact details and tell them that Ludo would get back to them. But this was a detective inspector. That would surely take priority.

'Well, my husband does keep some of the more valuable items locked in a secure vault in the cellar. Would you like to see those?'

'Yes, please, madam. I should like to take a look . . .'

'I take it you have a warrant?' Ludovic had come in, unheard, by the side door.

'No, I haven't, Mr de Coleville but . . .'

'Then I think you'd better come back when you have.' Ludovic took the barely touched coffee from Ash's hand and held the door open for him to leave.

After the policeman was safely out of earshot, Ludovic rounded on Sasha. 'What on earth did you think you were doing, you stupid woman? What did I tell you about not letting anyone look at the paintings in the vault — never mind showing them to the police!'

Sasha faltered. 'I'm sorry, Ludo, I thought it would be all right . . .'

'No, Sasha, you didn't think. Sometimes, I don't believe you have anything to think with. Well, I can't deal with you right now. I have work to do and it won't wait.'

Once outside, Ludovic drove his Range Rover around to the back entrance of the gallery. He'd decided against using the liveried de Coleville van which was custom-designed to transport paintings. He loaded half a dozen paintings without frames into the back — including a watercolour by Paul Klee, a couple of Matisse nudes and some rather alarming melting clocks by Dalí. All excellent and saleable forgeries. He needed somewhere to hide them until he could get them transported to Slater's Gallery. He had to think fast because he was in no doubt that the copper would be straight back with his damned warrant. As he drove down the high street, he had a brainwave. Jericho's shack was closed up and abandoned. No one had yet come to empty the detritus that he had no doubt it contained.

He broke in by the simple method of taking a tyre lever to the padlock at the back. Inside, the place reeked of rum and cannabis. Among the clothes and music paraphernalia, was a rack full of posters — scenes of Jamaica and portraits of reggae artists. Perfect. Ludovic stacked the paintings carefully in among them and covered them with gaudy Caribbean T-shirts and scarves. Now he would deal with Sasha.

In his haste to shift the forged paintings, Ludovic failed to notice that he was being tailed by a battered old saloon. After their meeting, Vince Parker had decided it might be advisable if he knew where this bloke hung out. He always liked to know the whereabouts of anyone who owed him money. He had the address of the Coleville Gallery but it didn't hurt to make sure. He watched with interest as Ludovic loaded the paintings, covered with a sheet, into the back of his car. He was even more intrigued when Ludovic broke into the back of the market stall and carried them inside. Parker's trained nose smelled a crooked deal — he'd been involved in plenty in his time. He took some photographs. There was money to be made here, if he played it right.

Later, back at the gallery, Banerjee returned with a warrant. Convinced there was something to find, and that de Coleville hadn't had time to shift it, he deployed his entire fraud team, with backup from the MIT. They turned over every inch of the gallery, including the opened vault, which now contained little of interest. Ludovic watched, calmly sipping single malt and smirking, while they searched. When they finally gave up and left, neither de Coleville nor Banerjee's fraud team noticed the battered blue hatchback parked opposite and the scruffy driver, with a grey ponytail, taking photographs.

CHAPTER EIGHT

'Did Big Ron do a post-mortem on poor old Jericho?' Corrie wondered. She was making corned beef hash for a late supper. It was Jack's favourite and when he'd finally arrived home, he'd looked like he needed some comforting nursery food.

'I doubt it,' he said, sinking into an armchair. 'No need. Jericho was being treated for all sorts of problems. Dr Griffin said he had a weak heart and given his lifestyle, he could have gone at any time but even so, he'd believed he had a few more years, yet. There were no suspicious circumstances, though. His death wasn't unexplained and there was no violence. Waste of public money to involve Big Ron, and you know what Garwood thinks about that.'

'Big Ron' was the nickname they had for Dr Veronica Hardacre — the indomitable but much-respected pathologist. She was a big-boned woman, strong and muscular, with bristling black eyebrows and a moustache to match. She had little time for senior police officers who considered themselves more important than the due process of science and made no exceptions, regardless of rank. Her predilection for sturdy knickers was legendary. Few members of the MIT had escaped a glimpse when she bent over to examine a dead body. Bugsy couldn't decide which was more traumatizing — a grisly corpse or a flash of Big Ron's drawers.

'Has George Garwood said anything to you about Cynthia's "at home"?' asked Corrie.

Garwood had every confidence that he would reach the rank of Commissioner before he retired. He told his wife, Cynthia, that she would be required to entertain luminaries such as High Court judges, cabinet ministers and often their wives, too. She guessed it wouldn't hurt to practise the correct etiquette for such bun fights, so that she'd know the ropes, if the time came.

'What's an "at home" when it's at home?' Jack sniggered at his own quip.

'It's a frightfully superior tea party for distinguished, upper-class guests.'

'Have you been invited?'

Corrie giggled. 'Good heavens, no. It's for elegant ladies — not kitchen fodder, like me. I'm just providing the food. She's ordered lots of expensive cream cakes and tiny triangular sandwiches. No cheap stuff or anything that looks like it came out of a Mr Kipling box — her words, not mine.' Corrie crushed some boiled potatoes — excellent Maris Pipers from the fruit and veg stall on the market. 'How has your day been, sweetheart? You look exhausted.'

'Bugsy and I had the dubious pleasure of riding shotgun for the Arts and Antiques lads, while they turned over the Coleville Gallery.'

'Really? I can't imagine a counterfeit *Mona Lisa* in the same location as *Lady on a Swing*. That's the painting hanging in their window at the moment. Very twee. How is the MIT involved?'

'We aren't, really. George Garwood offered our support to impress the commander, while things are quiet on the murder front. Detective Inspector Banerjee got a warrant to search the premises because he was positive there was something crooked going on. De Coleville had behaved very suspiciously when he'd first visited.'

'Did you find anything?'

'Not a dicky bird. Well, not unless you count a drawing of a cross-eyed sparrow that looks like it was done by a hyperactive chimpanzee with a crayon. It was entitled *Bird with Willow Twig* and the price tag was five thousand pounds. I reckon that's a crime in itself.'

'No forgeries, though.' Corrie served supper and put the brown sauce in front of her husband. She didn't really approve of shop-bought sauces in plastic bottles, but Jack thought corned beef hash wasn't the same without it.

'Apparently not. Banerjee was well annoyed. Ludovic de Coleville strutted about, smirking, while we searched. He was full of himself and kept making derogatory remarks about the totally unnecessary waste of public money and police harassment.'

'He's a bit arrogant at the best of times. Carlene says he occasionally goes into Corrie's Kitchen for some takeaway meals — always when she's just about to close. He behaves as if she should be grateful that he's buying food from her.'

'His wife seemed very nervous. Ash said she had been very pleasant and cooperative when he'd first arrived but as soon as Ludovic came home, she became very agitated. He reckoned there might be some coercive control going on.'

'I wonder why she stays with him?'

'Good question. She's very glamorous — long blonde hair and a smashing figure. It's probably about the money. He drives a top of the range SUV and his suit looked like he had the same tailor as James Bond, so he must be worth a few quid.'

Corrie put down her fork. 'Do you wish I had long blonde hair and a smashing figure?'

Jack recognized that deceptively innocent expression. A wrong answer at this point could mean his supper ending up in the bin. 'Why would I? You have the figure of a chef who believes in her own food. I bet Sasha de Coleville couldn't make corned beef hash like this.'

* * *

Despite his nonchalant manner, Ludovic was seriously shaken by the unwanted attention of the Art and Antiques Fraud Unit. He phoned Rob Slater for advice.

'I'm worried, Rob — very worried. That copper was standing right above the vault in the cellar where I'd stashed the merchandise. My stupid wife was about to take him in and give him a guided tour. Luckily, I was able to buy some time and shift the paintings while he went away to get a search warrant.'

'Christ, Ludo. What did you do with them? I trust they're somewhere safe.'

'Not really. I didn't have much time. I hid them inside a market stall — it's more of a shack, really — down the far end of the street. It's just a temporary measure.'

'What happens if the stallholder finds them?'

'He won't. He was an elderly Jamaican with an unhealthy lifestyle. He died of a heart attack. I believe the council boarded it up and padlocked it. I had to break in.'

Rob Slater guessed that Ludo was panicking. When people panic, they make mistakes. Sometimes, these mistakes implicate others and if Ludo went down, Rob had no intention of going down with him. There were some dangerous men waiting for those paintings and a lot of money was at stake. On the other hand, money wouldn't be much use to him if he went to jail for an indeterminate number of years. There would be other deals.

'Get rid of the stuff, Ludo. I know these Art Fraud coppers — they're smart and they know what they're looking at. Once they recognize fakes and identify a connection to organized-crime gangs, they never give up.'

Ludovic was sweating. 'That's what I thought. I'll destroy the paintings. Somehow. Leave it to me.'

'And while you're about it, you should offload your wife before she finds out what you're up to and gets you arrested. You've got the evidence you wanted — face her with it and chuck her out. It should be simple.'

* * *

When Parker turned up at the gallery for his money, Ludovic was anxious to pay him off and get rid of him. He was confident that David Wilson didn't pose any kind of threat, no matter what Sasha might tell him. He had no more use for the private eye and he was lowering the tone of the gallery with his scruffy clothes and ridiculous, greasy ponytail. He handed over the cash.

'I think you'll find that's right, Mr Parker. Thank you for your services. Good day to you.'

But Vince was in no hurry to leave. 'Not so fast, Mr de Coleville. I thought you might be interested to see these.' He produced photographs he'd taken of Ludovic hiding the paintings and later, of the police, searching the gallery. 'I'm guessing you've been a bit naughty — looks like bent merchandise to me. What are they, stolen or forgeries?'

Ludovic went cold. 'I don't know what you're talking about.'

'But these photos clearly show you breaking in and hiding what look like paintings, under a sheet. Then the filth shows up and spends an hour turning over your gaff. Now, what would you think was occurring, if you were me?'

'You'd better leave before I lose my temper.' Ludovic was fighting the urge to punch the grubby little creep on the jaw.

'All right. I'm going. But you'd better think about cutting me in to whatever deal you're planning. You wouldn't want someone to tip off the police about where you've hidden the stuff, would you? And before you do anything silly, these photographs are safely stored on my computer.'

'How dare you threaten me! You're a low-life sewer rat who preys on human depravity.'

Vince grinned. 'Save it, mate — I've heard it from experts.' He opened the door. 'I'll be in touch. Be lucky!'

He slouched out leaving Ludovic furious and scared at the same time. He wished he'd never taken Slater's advice to use the man. He took out his phone.

'Rob? It's Ludo. I've had a very unpleasant visit from your private investigator. He's been snooping into my affairs

— and I don't just mean my wife's sordid little affair, I mean *our* affairs. He's threatening to show some incriminating photographs to the police if we don't cut him in. What do we do?'

Rob Slater thought about it but only for a second. 'Calm down, Ludo. I'll deal with it. I know people who are expert at making a problem disappear without a trace.'

CHAPTER NINE

After Vince left the gallery, he wondered exactly how much the bent merchandise might be worth. He was no art expert, but it wouldn't hurt to take a look, and maybe get a few photographs. He could show them to a mate of his who'd handled a few stolen paintings in his time, then he'd know how much to demand as his cut. He drove down the high street until he came to the boarded-up shack where he had witnessed de Coleville break in and stash the stuff. It was padlocked again — more securely this time. Vince looked around to make sure no one was watching, then cut it off with the bolt cutters that he kept in the car. They came in handy when he needed to get inside lock-ups and the like, for closer surveillance.

Once inside, he closed the door behind him and pushed a box of Jericho's stock against it, in case anyone got nosey. The smell told him the previous occupant had been a heavy weed smoker. Nothing wrong with that, in his view. Whatever gets you through. Vince sat down in the battered armchair that had been Jericho's and picked up the half-empty bottle of rum that stood on the floor beside it. Well, why not? He'd have a few swigs while he searched. He found a tin of fat joints next to the rum and sniffed one. He reckoned these would be good ganja — the best. He found some matches in his pocket and lit up.

He rummaged through a heap of Rastafarian shirts, baggy trousers and knitted hats but there was nothing. Then he spotted the rack with the posters. Pulling off the sheet that covered them, he found prints of Bob Marley, Delroy Wilson, Jimmy Cliff and other reggae musicians. The idyllic scenes of Caribbean beaches boasted soft white sand, tranquil blue waters and picture-perfect weather, all year round. Vince reckoned that with the money he was going to make out of this caper, he might just spend a month or two there.

He finished off the rum and lit another joint. Finally, he found what he was looking for — the moody oil paintings. They looked genuine to him but obviously they weren't. This is what would earn him a shedload of loot. He took out his phone to take some pictures but suddenly, he was finding it difficult to focus. His head was swimming. This Jamaican shit must be stronger than he thought. Briefly, he wondered if, instead of taking photographs, he should pinch the paintings and stash them in the boot of his car. He could use them to put pressure on that poncey de Coleville. Yes, that's what he'd do. Safer to have the real thing, even if they were fakes.

He tried to stand up then promptly sat back down again. Everything around him was spinning and the dizziness was getting worse. He felt sick but he daren't throw up. He'd worn gloves to avoid fingerprints but the cops could get your DNA from vomit. He knew they already had both on his file. When he did manage to push himself upright, his legs gave way, weak and trembling. He doubted he'd be able to drive and wondered if he should even try. The decision was made for him. He passed out cold on the heap of Rasta shirts.

* * *

Under cover of darkness, Ludovic de Coleville drove down to the insalubrious end of the high street and parked his car as far from Jericho's shack as he dared. He waited a few

49

interminable minutes while a random dog walker came past and disappeared up a side-turning. He'd dressed carefully — black trousers, a black jacket with deep pockets and a ski-mask over his head with just his eyes, nose and mouth exposed. Even if someone saw him, he'd be impossible to identify with any certainty. A little melodramatic, possibly, but he must destroy the forgeries. Without them as evidence, there was little the police could do. He doubted Parker would want to have dealings with coppers, despite his blackmail threats. That's if he was still around after Slater had ensured his silence. He envied Slater. The man had gravitas. OK, his taste in suits was a little flamboyant for Ludovic's taste but the George Michael shades were awesome. He planned to get some for himself.

He climbed out of his car and opened the boot. The petrol can was full. He took it out and felt for the blowtorch in his jacket pocket. That had been a lucky find. Just what he needed to do the job. Someone had removed the padlock he'd fixed to the door. Kids, probably — breaking in to nick the shirts and CDs. No matter. It would make his job easier. He needed to work fast. He didn't need to go right inside, just far enough to ensure the whole place was thoroughly doused in petrol. As soon as the can was empty, he went back outside. Petrol was dangerous stuff. A friend of his had been badly burned, just sloshing a bit on his barbecue. He stood well back, lit the blowtorch, pressed the lock button, then tossed it in through the open door. The whole place exploded in flames and he watched from a distance, as it burned. Satisfied that nothing would remain when the fire was out, he sprinted to his car and drove home. Someone must have called the fire service because as he reached the Coleville Gallery, two fire engines sped past with lights blazing and sirens blaring.

* * *

It was much later that night when the call came through to DI Dawes. It was the crew commander of the fire service.

'At first, it seemed like a simple case of mindless arson — possibly some local youth, hanging about at night, looking for mischief. Then we found the remains of a body. I think this is one for you, Jack.'

DI Dawes and DC Williams were first at the scene. SOCOs had set up powerful lights and Dr Hardacre was already there. She was kneeling beside the body, kitted out in full white coveralls to reduce the risk of contamination. She stood up.

'He's a bit crisp at present, gentlemen, so I can't tell you much until I get him back to the mortuary.'

'The body is that of a male, though, Doctor?' Jack caught his breath. The smell of petrol was still overpowering and everywhere was soaking wet and dripping from the fire service hoses.

'Yes, I can be sure of that. I've had a poke about but I've found nothing to identify him. It must have been bloody hot — even the soles of his trainers have melted. I'm hoping I shall be able to get some DNA from bone matter. If not, it will have to be a dental records job, although from the look of what's left of his teeth, he wasn't too worried about dental hygiene.'

'Would he have been conscious after the place caught fire?' asked DC Williams.

'Well, what do you think, constable? You walk into a petrol-fuelled explosion, you don't get up and walk out again. He'd have been killed instantly by the blast. I can't even be certain whether he was alive or dead, when it went up. From the position of the body, there's a possibility that he was either asleep or drunk, before he was barbecued. As I said, I'll know more when I've been able to analyse what's left of the poor devil.'

Jack and Aled turned to leave, to let the SOCO team get on with their work. A suspicious death, certainly — unexplained, temporarily. Whoever had doused Jericho's shack with petrol and started the fire had intended it, and its contents, to burn to the ground. The issue was whether they had known there was someone in there and went ahead anyway, or was the victim simply collateral damage. It was the job of the MIT to find out.

'Detective Inspector Dawes, the crew commander thought you should see this.' The young officer held out an evidence bag. 'He believes it's what was used to set the petrol alight.'

Jack took the bag. Inside were the remains of the blowtorch that Ludovic had thrown in, setting off the massive explosion. Jack turned it over in his hand. Surely not. He looked closer. The dents were unmistakeable. Even though it had suffered in the blaze, the metal handle was intact. Unless it was a massive coincidence — and Jack didn't believe in coincidences — this was Corrie's blowtorch. He had watched her use it many times to caramelize crème brulée. Now, it seemed it had been instrumental in killing someone. He needed to find out how she had lost it and, more importantly, who might have found it.

CHAPTER TEN

Right, Fen, here's the plunger thingy, ready loaded.' Judith handed it over and Fenella took it in finger and thumb, as if it were red hot. 'You say Ida always has toast and jam for breakfast.'

'That's right. She comes prancing down in her fancy dressing gown — she calls it a *peignoir* — like the lady of the manor and plonks herself down at the table, opposite David. I have to bring her toast, in the toast rack, with the butter dish and a pot of the strawberry jam that I make for our Ladies' Guild stall. She says shop-bought jam tastes cheap and is full of pulp, instead of fruit.'

Judith had a sudden thought. 'Does David have jam on his toast?'

'No.' Fenella was adamant. 'He says it's too sweet for breakfast. He only has Seville marmalade.'

'OK, so here's what we're going to do. Get up earlier than usual. Get a fresh pot of jam from the batch you've set aside for the stall. Take off the cover and paper disc, then take out a spoonful of the jam and bin it. Squirt in the anti-freeze and mix it with the jam on top. Then put the lid back on, so it looks like a new, untouched jar. Wipe it clean of fingerprints and put it where you usually keep it, so as not to raise any suspicion. When you take in the toast and butter, say that you've forgotten the jam and ask David to get it.'

'That way, his fingerprints will be on it if anything should go wrong,' said Fenella.

'Exactly. Then you go out. Say that you're shopping for something nice for Ida's supper and leave them to have their breakfast. Take the plunger with you. When you cross the bridge on the way to the shopping centre, drop it in the river.'

Fenella nodded enthusiastically. 'I'll be out of the house when she hyperventilates and has a heart attack — a real one, this time. David won't take much notice at first because he knows she puts it on, even though he won't admit it.'

'By the time he realizes she's genuinely ill . . .' began Judith,

' . . . it'll be too late,' finished Fenella.

If luck had been on their side, it should have gone like clockwork. But fate had other ideas.

* * *

Fenella had lain awake most of the night, thinking about what she had to do in the morning. Only the blissful thought of a life without Ida kept her strong and determined. As Jude had told her: you can't make an omelette without breaking a few eggs in the process. She had gone over the plan in her head a million times. She had to get every aspect of it right. When her alarm went off at six, she got up, showered and dressed and went down to the kitchen. The house was silent. Too early for either David or Ida to make an appearance. That was good. Things were going according to plan.

In the outside store cupboard, where she kept items that were destined for the Ladies' Guild stall, there was a tray of twelve pots of strawberry jam. Carefully, she took one out and removed the lid and paper disc. She had the plunger of ethylene glycol in her pocket. She scooped out a spoonful of jam and looked around for somewhere to dispose of it but there wasn't anywhere. She didn't want to take it back to the kitchen and she needed to get rid of it where nobody would find it and wonder why it was wasted. On a sudden impulse, she ate it. Then she squirted in the poison, just as Jude had instructed, and mixed it in using the empty spoon. Once she had replaced the paper disc, she put back the red, gingham jam pot cover and secured it with a rubber band. It looked exactly like the others — nothing at all suspicious.

Back in the kitchen, she wiped the jar clean of finger-prints and placed it in the cupboard, alongside the other jams and David's marmalade. She put the spoon in the dishwasher, already half full from last night's supper, and switched it on. Done! Now she could stop shaking. She made herself a strong cup of coffee. By the time she'd drunk it, it was eight o'clock. David and Ida would be down soon. She started making toast.

By the time they put in an appearance, Fenella had prac-tised what she would say, over and over in her mind.

'Good morning,' she said brightly. 'Looks like it's going to be a nice day. I thought I'd get your breakfasts, then pop into town for some of those sausages you like for supper, Ida. They sell out very quickly.'

'I don't want sausages,' Ida retorted immediately.

'What would you like, dear?' asked David. 'I'm sure Fenella will get it for you.'

'Yes, of course.' Fenella smiled through gritted teeth. Any qualms she'd felt about poisoning the old bitch vanished instantly. 'What do you fancy?' She could tell Ida was racking her brains for the most inconvenient and obscure ingredients that would take ages to find, and even longer to prepare and cook. Fenella didn't mind as she had no intention of buying them. The old bag could ask for peacock's brains, for all she cared.

'I want beef olives with a balsamic glaze,' announced Ida, finally. 'Fillet of beef, mind, not some cheap bit of brisket from the market that you've bashed flat with a meat mallet. And with them, I'd like artichokes stuffed with parmesan and breadcrumbs. I'm sure you'll find some, if you look properly.'

'Certainly, Ida. No trouble at all.' Fenella put the toast rack and plates on the table, then went back for the butter dish and marmalade. 'David, I've forgotten your mother's strawberry jam. Would you mind fetching it for her, darling?'

'That's right,' taunted Ida, 'get your husband to fetch and carry for you. He has a full day's work ahead of him, not waltzing around town, window-shopping.'

'It's all right, Mother,' said David. He couldn't face yet another row at this time of the morning. 'I'll get it.' He came back with the jam and put it in front of Ida.

Fenella stared at it in terrible fascination then dragged her eyes away. So far, everything was going to plan. She braced herself. 'Right, I'll be off then. See you later.'

'I'll be working late tonight, Fenella. It's Friday and I have the company accounts to check.' David had arranged an assignation with Sasha. They were going to a romantic hotel he had found, well out in the country.

'That's fine,' said Fenella. 'I'll keep you some supper.' *Except you won't want it*, she thought with morbid pleasure. *You'll be watching the funeral directors cart your mother off and dump her miserable, rancid carcass in a coffin.*

* * *

Fenella walked into town as planned. As she went over the Richington Bridge, she took the now-empty syringe out of her pocket and casually dropped it into the river. Then she found a teashop and ordered a pot of tea. She sat and sipped it until her hands had stopped shaking, then she phoned Judith.

'It's done, Jude. How long should I wait before I go home and find the body?'

'I'd give it a couple of hours at least. You don't want to get home and find she's still breathing her last. Did you see her actually eat the jam?'

'No, but she will have done. The pot was on the table with David's prints on it, just in case there's any trouble.'

'Good girl. Is David likely to get home before you?'

'No, he's working late. It's the company accounts. I doubt if he'll be home before eleven. He's been working late quite a lot, recently.'

'Then you'll need to phone him, when you find Ida. Tell him he has to come home, his poor mother has had a fatal heart attack. You need to sound tearful and shocked. Can you do that?'

'Yes. I think so.'

'Right. Message me later, when all the fuss has died down.'

* * *

It was five o'clock, when Fenella finally arrived home. She had treated herself to a very tasty lunch at Chez Carlene, then gone to the cinema. She wasn't sure what she'd seen — she hadn't really been paying attention — but she vaguely remembered women in long Regency dresses, with their waistlines high up under their bosoms. She supposed she should remember something of it, in case she needed to account for her whereabouts at the time of Ida's death.

Tentatively, she unlocked the front door and went in. Out of habit, she called out, 'Hello! I'm home.'

'And about time, too!' It was Ida's voice from the drawing room. Fenella nearly fainted. She clutched the hall stand to steady herself. What on earth had gone wrong?

'Ida?' she called, her voice shaking. 'Is that you?'

'Of course it is. Who were you expecting, the Queen of Sheba? I've been waiting for hours. I need you to cut my toenails. Did you get my beef olives and artichokes?' Ida glanced at Fenella's ashen face. 'No, of course you didn't. You can't do anything right, can you?'

She went into one of her long, acrimonious tirades but Fenella wasn't listening. She hurried into the kitchen, without taking off her coat. In the cupboard, where she kept the jam, there were half-eaten pots of blackcurrant and raspberry

57

and David's Seville marmalade, but the jar of strawberry jam wasn't there. Knowing that Ida was capable of eating most of a pot for breakfast and finishing it off on scones for tea, she looked in the bin for an empty jar. There wasn't one. Where the hell was it? And why wasn't Ida dead? Panicking now, she returned to the drawing room where Ida was still complaining, hardly noticing that her daughter-in-law had left the room.

Fenella interrupted the diatribe. 'Ida, did you finish that jar of strawberry jam that David fetched for you this morning?'

Ida's tone was belligerent. 'Why do you need to know? Are you going to keep a count of everything I eat, now?'

'No, it's just that David doesn't always remember to keep empty jars to be sterilised for more jam. He sometimes puts them in the glass recycling.' *Why can't you just answer the question, you vile old crow?*

'If you must know, I didn't fancy strawberry this morning, so David took it away and fetched me a pot of blackcurrant instead. He's such a good son, nothing is too much trouble.'

Fenella felt a terrible rush of nausea. Bile rose in her throat. 'What did he do with the pot of strawberry, Ida? It isn't in the cupboard with the rest of the jam.'

'I've no idea. You'd have to ask him, although I don't think he should be bothered with such trivia. He's a busy man. I doubt your silly drawings bring in much money, so he has to work long hours to keep you — God knows why. Now, are you going to cut my toenails or not?'

Right at that moment, Fenella could have cheerfully cut Ida's throat. She couldn't leave it there. There was a pot of poisoned jam somewhere, capable of killing someone innocent. She wouldn't rest until she found it. She went to her bedroom, out of Ida's earshot. She phoned David but his personal assistant said he'd left the office at lunchtime and no, he hadn't told her anything about working late on the accounts. Desperate now, Fenella tried his mobile. It went straight to answerphone.

Sobbing, she phoned Judith. 'Jude, it didn't work, she didn't eat it and now the jam's gone missing and so has David. I don't know what to do.'

'Fen, you're not making sense. Tell me exactly what happened.'

Fenella went through everything that had happened, since she'd phoned from the teashop. Judith listened in silence. 'You need to stay focused, Fen. There are two things that are important right now. First, you have to find out from David what he did with the jam and destroy it. Don't make a big thing of it, just casually ask. Then, we need to think of something else sweet that Ida likes, so we can put the poison in that. She may well be suspicious of jam, now.'

'Yes, OK.' Fenella gulped. 'It will be all right, won't it, Jude?'

'Of course it will. Trust me,' replied Judith, with a confidence that she was far from feeling.

CHAPTER ELEVEN

David and Sasha had dined extravagantly and were now enjoying coffee and cognac on the terrace of Kingston Country Club.

'That was a wonderful dinner, darling.' Sasha reached out and took David's hand. 'The duck was superb.'

'Yes, they can usually knock out a decent meal here.' He thought Sasha looked especially stunning tonight. She was wearing a simple but elegant summer dress in sapphire silk that matched her eyes and set off her gleaming blonde hair. *Mother's right*, he thought, *I should probably have married Sasha*. If only Fenella had tried harder to please him, made more effort to look attractive, like a wife should, he thought their marriage might have stood a chance. The constant sniping about their lack of children and how it was his mother's fault irritated him hugely. Why should a man be judged on his ability to breed? His affair with Sasha had given him a reason — if he needed one — to move on. He poured more coffee. 'Where does Ludovic think you are tonight?'

'He didn't ask and I didn't tell him. He's too busy with the gallery and making money to care about me.'

'Never mind, sweetheart. I'll pick you up tomorrow afternoon and we'll spend the whole night together. You'd like that, wouldn't you?'

'That would be wonderful, David.'

* * *

Back at the Coleville Gallery, Ludovic was fitting out the cellar with tighter security. He was expecting delivery of some fine examples of fake Chinese porcelain the following day, which would make him a huge profit. Trying to get such forgeries genuinely appraised and valued was nigh on impossible, unless the pieces were blindingly obvious, and these were all excellent. He needed to keep them safe until he could pass them on to Slater. He doubted Banerjee would be granted a second warrant so soon after he'd searched and found nothing, unless he could find new evidence, and Ludovic intended to ensure that he didn't. The threats from Parker had unnerved him, briefly, but he'd heard nothing from the grubby little man, so concluded that he'd thought better of trying blackmail. If he did surface, he'd let Slater's men deal with him.

In truth, now that Ludovic knew it was Weedy Wilson that Sasha was seeing, he was unconcerned. Wilson, in his view, was an ineffective milksop, with neither the wits nor the backbone to be any kind of threat to his forgery business. As far as he was concerned, if he wanted Sasha, he could have her. She'd be up for grabs very shortly, anyway, as he'd now started divorce proceedings.

* * *

By the time David came home, very late, Fenella was desperate. She had searched the entire house, the garden and all the outside bins at least twice. Neither the jam nor its empty pot was anywhere to be found. She had planned to follow Jude's

61

advice to ask him, casually, what he'd done with it, but the minute he walked through the door, she confronted him. She couldn't help herself.

'David, I need to speak to you. It's important.'

Ida called to him from upstairs. 'David, will you tell Fenella she has to cut my toenails. She won't do it and I'm sure one of them has started to grow inwards. It's very painful but she doesn't care.'

'Ida, be quiet!' Fenella shouted back. 'I need to speak to David without your constant interruptions.'

'Well, I beg your pardon, I'm sure.' Ida was shocked as Fenella was usually so docile and compliant. 'I hadn't realized I can't speak to my own son when I want to. I suppose you think I should wait my turn.' She carried on grumbling to herself but Fenella shut the drawing room door so she couldn't be heard.

'What do you want to say that's so important that you need to be rude to Mother?' asked David. He was thinking fast, suspecting that Fenella had found out about Sasha. He had expected his wife and mother to have gone to bed hours ago and he'd intended to shower before Fenella could smell Sasha's perfume on him. He wondered how best to handle the situation. Was she going to ask for a divorce? He wondered where that would leave him. The house was hers, so presumably she could ask him to leave and take Ida with him. He wasn't sure what his rights were. Or his mother's, come to that. He reproached himself for not having consulted a solicitor before now.

Fenella took a deep breath and tried to sound more relaxed. 'It's about your mother's strawberry jam.'

'What? Do you mean to tell me you're making all this fuss about jam, at this time of night?' Inwardly, he breathed a sigh of relief. He had been sure that she was about to ask why he'd told her he was working late when he'd left the office at lunchtime. He knew she'd phoned and his secretary had told her. He'd seen several missed calls from her on his phone, and he'd planned to tell her he'd switched it off, so he could concentrate on what he was doing. It was true, in a way.

Fenella tried again. 'Ida said that after I left this morning, she decided she didn't want strawberry jam, so you took it away and brought her a pot of blackcurrant.'

'Yes, that's right, but why—'

'What did you do with it, David?' She was trying very hard to keep her voice level but it came out high-pitched and shrill.

'I can't remember. Does it matter?'

'Yes, of course it matters.' She thrashed around for a good reason. 'We can't waste jam on a whim of your mother's. It makes money for the Ladies' Guild stall.' It sounded lame but it was the best she could do on the spur of the moment.

'Now you've reminded me what I did with it. Mother said she was tired of strawberry jam and wasn't likely to eat it any time soon. It hadn't been touched, so I put it back in the tray in the outside store cupboard, where you keep the ones you've set aside for your stall There was an empty place for it in the tray and it had the same red-checked cover as the others. You don't need to worry, nothing has been wasted. I think I'll have a shower before bed, then my mug of Ovaltine.' He turned and went upstairs before she could ask any more questions or get a whiff of Sasha's perfume.

Fenella almost sprinted outside to the store cupboard. The tray wasn't there. It hadn't been there when she'd searched earlier. It had vanished — together with the poisoned jar. She went back inside the house and poured herself a stiff, medicinal brandy.

* * *

Next morning, Fenella prepared breakfast almost in a daze. She'd spent most of the night imagining a variety of scenarios that would explain the missing tray of jam. Perhaps someone had broken in and stolen it. Maybe Ida had been poking around in there and knocked it to the floor. She would have got rid of the evidence rather than own up. But where would she have disposed of all the sticky, broken glass? Fenella's night terrors became more and more bizarre as time wore on. Next-door's dog had got in there and dragged the tray off to its kennel. Gangs of feral children, roaming the streets, took it away and ate it. Finally, she fell into a fitful sleep plagued with nightmares about being held responsible for poisoning all the dogs and children in the neighbourhood.

'You're looking more haggard than usual this morning, Fenella,' observed David.

Thank you for that, darling. 'I didn't sleep very well, that's all.'

'I'm sure you got more sleep than I did,' complained Ida. 'I barely shut my eyes all night, my toe throbbed so much. It wouldn't surprise me if sepsis has set in. I could drop dead and you wouldn't care.'

With a bit of luck, that's exactly what you'll do. 'So the snoring I heard coming from your room wasn't you?' Fenella wasn't in the mood for Ida's sniping.

Ida sniffed. 'I never snore.'

'I suppose, as it's Saturday, you'll be off to the market this morning,' said David.

'Yes, I suppose I shall.' Fenella needed to speak to Judith urgently.

David looked at the newspaper, rather than meet Fenella's gaze. He chose his words carefully. 'Some of the blokes from work have planned a fishing trip today. We're going to fish the Thames around Teddington. I expect we'll have some supper afterwards and a few drinks, so I shan't be home tonight. We'll find a pub somewhere. If you wanted to, you could stay with your friend from the Ladies' Guild again.'

'No, she couldn't,' said Ida, instantly. 'Someone has to be here to look after me. I'm too frail to be left alone. And speaking of the Ladies' Guild, Fenella, I forgot to tell you. One of the women called while you were out yesterday. She wanted to know if you had any jam for the stall. I told her where you kept it and she took a tray of strawberry away with her.'

Without a word to anyone, Fenella grabbed her coat and hurried down to the market. It was bustling already, with shoppers making an early start on food for the weekend. The Ladies' Guild stall was being run by Joyce and Margaret — a couple of newish recruits. They were doing a roaring trade already. Fenella slipped behind the stall and looked for the tray of strawberry jam. All she found was the empty tray, put aside for disposal. There were no jars on the counter.

'Joyce, where's the strawberry jam?'

Joyce smiled. 'Hello, Mrs Wilson. I met your mother-in-law, Mrs Wilson senior, yesterday, when I came to pick it up. What a lovely old dear. But what are you doing here so early? I didn't think you were on the rota to take over until this afternoon.'

'I'm not. I just thought I'd pop in to see if you needed any help.' Fenella asked again, really anxious now. 'Where are the twelve jars of strawberry jam that you collected from my home yesterday?'

'We haven't any left. Your jam is always a favourite. They were all sold out half an hour ago. Good, isn't it?'

Wonderful, thought Fenella. *Just bloody wonderful. Someone in Kings Richington has bought a pot of lethal strawberry jam and we've no idea who it is.*

CHAPTER TWELVE

When Jack got home, Corrie wasn't there. She'd left a note saying that she and Carlene were out working at the Cuisine's kitchen unit. Cynthia Garwood's 'posh nosh' garden party was the following afternoon and they were preparing the cakes and tarts to get ahead of themselves before delivery the next day. The sandwiches would be made fresh just before the event.

Jack wondered how best to ask her about the blowtorch. He didn't imagine for one moment that she had anything to do with the fire in Jericho's shack, but she may have important information about who did. Forensics had tested the torch for fingerprints and anything else that might help with identification but had drawn a blank. The extreme heat had all but melted it. The familiar dents, however, remained distinct.

'Hello, Jack.' Corrie was surprised to see him. 'What brings you here to our den of decadent dining?'

'Before you pinch one of those chocolate éclairs, Mr Jack, I've counted them,' joked Carlene.

'It all looks delicious,' said Jack. 'Much too good for old Garwood and his cronies.'

Corrie grinned. 'I don't think men are invited. As I understand it from Cynthia, she's providing tea for her charity-committee ladies. No doubt it's in preparation for when George gets promoted to Lord High Executioner and she has to entertain the Lord High Everything Else — Sir Barnaby Featherstonehaugh, and his scary wife, Lady Lobelia. We may get more business from it.'

'Are you doing any caramelizing today?' Jack began, carefully.

Corrie sensed an agenda. 'That's a random question. Why do you ask?'

'Old Jericho's shack was burned down last night.'

'Yes, we heard, didn't we, Carlene?'

'Yeah. Who'd do a thing like that? Bad enough that the poor old sod's dead without destroying all his possessions. There are some right animals living round here.'

Jack frowned. 'According to the head of the fire crew, it was doused in petrol and set alight with a chef's blowtorch.'

'Are you questioning every chef who owns a culinary blowtorch?' asked Corrie. 'It'll take a long time. There must be hundreds of them.'

'Yes, but they don't all have triangular dents in the handgrip, like the ones I made in yours when I dropped it on the patio.'

Corrie stopped whipping cream and stared at him. 'But you don't think it's mine, surely? It can't possibly be. Where is it now? Can I see it?'

''Fraid not. It's locked up in the evidence room.'

'Well, mine's back home in the kitchen.'

Carlene bit her lip. 'Er — actually, no, it isn't, Mrs D. I borrowed it to caramelize some slices of tarte Tatin. The gas cylinder had run out on mine and I needed it in a hurry.'

After years of practice, Jack slipped effortlessly into interrogation mode. 'Where were you when you last used it?'

Carlene thought hard. 'Corrie's Kitchen. We were doing a special — a three-course takeaway meal for a tenner. Tarte Tatin was the dessert.'

'How did you lose it?' Jack was taking notes now.

'I left it on the counter while I packed up a takeaway in the back. We were very busy — customers in and out all evening. When I went to get it, it had gone.'

'Could someone have taken it, when you weren't looking?' suggested Jack, scribbling fast.

'Yeah, but why nick a blowtorch? If you wanted to burn down an old shack, you could do it with some newspaper and a box of matches.'

'Not really. Too dangerous when petrol's involved. It would need to be something you could chuck inside from a distance. A blowtorch would be ideal.'

'Yeah. Well, thank goodness no one was hurt,' said Carlene, with relief.

Corrie saw Jack's expression. 'Was somebody hurt, Jack? Is that why MIT is investigating?'

'I'm afraid so. After they put out the fire, the firemen found a body inside. Burned beyond recognition.'

'Bloody hell!' said Carlene. 'That's awful. And it's all my fault.'

'No, of course it isn't,' countered Corrie. 'Whoever did it could have found some other means of setting a fire. They just spotted your blowtorch and took advantage of the opportunity.'

And, thought Jack, *they obviously intended to destroy the whole place or they wouldn't have used petrol.* 'No chance of you remembering who came in that night?' he asked.

'No. I'm sorry, Mr Jack. The place was rammed all evening. If Tom Cruise had come in stark naked, with a doughnut round his wossisname, I wouldn't have noticed. Well . . . maybe I would. But I've no idea when it went missing. One minute it was there, then when I looked, it had gone. I meant to tell you, Mrs D, but we've been so busy, I forgot.' She had a sudden, frightening thought. 'Oh blimey! It'll have my fingerprints on it.'

'And mine,' said Corrie.

'Calm down, both of you. Forensics are still trying but so far, they haven't found any identifiable fingerprints due to the intense heat. If they do find any, we can soon eliminate you both from the enquiry. Tell me, Carlene, do your customers usually pay with bank cards?'

'Most of 'em, yes. Not many punters carry cash these days.'

'We could try tracing the card receipts from that night. It might give us a lead but it will be a long job. I'll get the team on to it.' Jack turned to go, relieved that there was an explanation for how Corrie's blowtorch had turned up at a crime scene. On his way out, he pinched a chocolate éclair, when Carlene wasn't looking.

* * *

The news of Jericho's stall burning down and the unidentified body found inside had reached the *Richington Echo* in record time. Never a fan of the police, the editor made great play of how slow Chief Superintendent Garwood and his minions had been at releasing details of the body. The editor was no fonder of the head of the local council and claimed that the shack, and its occupant, should have been removed months ago. It was an eyesore and contravened market regulations.

When Ludovic de Coleville saw the report, his initial reaction was horror. He'd had no idea that there had been someone inside when he torched the stall. Why hadn't they shouted when he was chucking petrol around? He concluded it had been a homeless person, sleeping rough and taking advantage of shelter. It explained why the padlock had been removed. That night had been very dark and there was no way he would have seen a comatose body, maybe drunk or drugged, unless he'd tripped over it. Anyway, it was too late now to do anything other than keep his head down. At least now he didn't have to worry about blasted Banerjee poking around. The photographs Vince Parker had taken of him stashing the forgeries were still a concern. They could link him to the fire, if the police got hold of them. But despite Parker's threats, there had been no sign of him — so far.

* * *

Jack and Corrie rarely phoned each other at work unless it was important, so when Jack's mobile rang and he saw it was Corrie, he was immediately concerned.

'Hello, love. Is there a problem?'

'Yes, Jack, there is. Would it be possible for you to come out to the unit?'

'What, right now?'

'Yes, please. If you can.' Corrie sounded upset, not at all like her usual confident self.

'OK. Give me half an hour to finish briefing the troops and I'll be there.'

The team had transferred their attention from cold cases to sifting through the card receipts from Corrie's Kitchen. It was a tedious job — the place had indeed been 'rammed' on the night in question, as Carlene had told him.

'I don't know if this is going to help us find out who nicked Mrs D's blowtorch from Carlene,' said Bugsy. 'Every bugger in Kings Richington seems to have bought grub there that night. Even Lady Lobelia. You wouldn't think the commander would send his wife out for a couple of ten-quid meal-deals, would you?'

'I doubt whether Sir Barnaby would dare to *send* Lady Lobelia anywhere. Corrie says she's her own woman and takes no prisoners. I'm not in the least surprised that they buy meals from Corrie's Kitchen. It's good food, good value and convenient if you don't feel like cooking. Carlene and her team are making a very good job of it. Listen, Bugsy, I've got to go out for a bit. Corrie just phoned and she sounded agitated — most unusual for her.'

'She all right, Jack? Do you want me to come with you, in case you need help?'

'No, it's OK, but thanks for the offer. I'll find out what's wrong and if I need you, I'll ring.'

When Jack got to Coriander's Cuisine, Corrie and Carlene were going through mounds of ingredients, spread out on the worktops.

'Jack, something dreadful has happened.' Corrie was clearly distraught. 'Do you remember me telling you about Cynthia Garwood's "at home"? Well, it was this afternoon. Carlene and I took the food over in the van and set it out on a table in the garden. It looked lovely — snowy white tablecloths, flowers and elegant food. She was very pleased. We left when the ladies began to arrive, then went back around five to collect the plates and cake stands.'

'It was awful, Mr Jack,' continued Carlene. 'I've seen some serious chucking up in my time. Well, you do, if you spend a lot of time in clubs. Some nights, in the ladies', you have to pick your way around puddles of it. But this was puke on an industrial level.'

Corrie nodded in agreement. 'Oh Jack, it was ghastly. The guests were staggering about the garden, throwing up in the flower beds and falling over on the grass. Only two ladies were unaffected and one of them had the presence of mind to call Dr Griffin. He reckoned it was food poisoning. He said none of them was ill enough to go to hospital but they needed to go home and rest and drink lots of water. Of course, Cynthia wasn't at all happy. In between vomiting, she claimed it had to be my food that caused it because they hadn't had anything else, only tea. I dare say that's true because I don't believe she's ever cooked anything in her life.'

'I can imagine she'd be a bit miffed,' said Jack. No doubt he'd be hearing all about it from the chief super.

'If it gets out that my food isn't safe, it'll ruin the business. People always believe the worst, even when there's no proof. And that's what I want you to do, Jack. You have to prove it wasn't my food.'

'But nobody died, Corrie. I can't get a murder team to investigate a case of food poisoning. Isn't that the job of the environmental health people on the council?'

'Noooo!' Corrie and Carlene chorused.

'It may come to that,' agreed Corrie, when she'd calmed down. 'But I'm certain my food didn't poison anyone. If I had any doubts at all, which I don't, it would probably be the sandwiches. They were smoked salmon and cream cheese and prawns with cucumber. I bought the fish from my usual supplier, it's always fine — but you never know with prawns. Some people are allergic. But we follow all the rules about allergen information and best practice as laid down by the Food Standards Agency, don't we Carlene?'

'We certainly do. I've had food-allergy training on every diet going — vegan, vegetarian, low fat, low carb, free-from, gluten-free, taste-free and a few more I'd never heard of. We display allergy and intolerance information on all our signs and menus and on packaged food. What more could we do?'

'I doubt if the ladies could all have the same allergies,' said Jack. 'It does sound more like food poisoning.'

'All I'm asking is that you to do an initial, unbiased check. Please, Jack.'

'Please, Mr Jack,' begged Carlene.

* * *

Jack took Bugsy when he went to see Cynthia Garwood. He didn't want it to look as if he was there as Corrie's husband, attempting to cover something up. And he knew Cynthia liked Bugsy — most ladies did. Cynthia had calmed down somewhat, now that she'd stopped being sick.

'Jack, this is ghastly. We were all so ill. I can't believe it had anything to do with Corrie's food. She's been catering my events for years and there has never been a hint of a problem. But what else could it have been?'

'Corrie is very upset, as you can imagine. Obviously, it isn't a police matter unless someone was trying to poison you on purpose, which I very much doubt. Bugsy and I thought we'd come along as friends, to see if we could get to the bottom of it.'

'Did all you ladies eat the same things?' asked Bugsy.

'More or less.' Cynthia was trying to remember. 'All the food was delicious and everyone tucked in.'

'But not everyone was sick.'

'No. Jessica and Pamela were fine. They were looking after the rest of us until the doctor came.'

'Can you remember if there was anything they didn't have — cakes, scones, sandwiches?' Jack knew that Corrie had been concerned about the fillings in some of the sandwiches.

'No, we all ate the same . . .' She hesitated. 'No, hang on a minute. Jess and Pam only had the sandwiches. They're on some sort of sugar-free, weight-watching thing. They made a point of saying the cakes and scones looked gorgeous but they weren't allowed to eat any.'

Well, thought Jack, *that exonerates the prawns.* 'And everything you ate came from Coriander's Cuisine? You didn't provide anything yourself?'

Cynthia smiled wryly. 'No, Jack, I wouldn't know where to start. That's why I rely on Corrie for anything special.'

'Have you got any of the party food left, Mrs Garwood?' asked Bugsy.

'No, it all went in the food bin and the council refuse men took it away. I didn't want George nibbling at it and getting sick. Or even worse, the dog. I'd be heartbroken if anything happened to him.'

'Yes, we're all very fond of Chief Superintendent Garwood,' lied Bugsy.

'Thanks, but I meant the dog.'

* * *

On the way back in the car, Bugsy was trying to think of a solution to what could become a big problem for Mrs D and Carlene. 'You don't think it could have been something in the tea, do you, Jack? I mean, she must at least have made the tea herself. Maybe it was something in the water or the milk was off.'

'I don't think sour milk would have caused such a spectacular bout of vomiting. I've heard of the water supply being poisoned by lead pipes, but in old houses, not one as grand as Garwood's. No, it has to have been something they ate.'

Bugsy grinned. 'I know it's serious, guv, but you can't help laughing. All those frosty-knickered, hoity-toity, ladies who lunch, stumbling around the garden in their high heels looking for a plant pot to spew in. Carlene said Lady Lobelia puked in the pond. It must've scared the shit out of the fish.'

'At least Mrs Garwood doesn't seem to want to sue or report anything. Trouble is, mud sticks. I can't believe some of those posh ladies won't gossip about it. The only thing that will help is if we can find out what caused it and prove that it's nothing to do with Corrie's food.'

CHAPTER THIRTEEN

The post-mortem on the burned body found in Jericho's Caribbean music shack was harrowing to say the least. Jack had intended that only he and Bugsy would attend — there was little about violent death that they hadn't already seen. But DC Williams and DC Fox were already in the mortuary room, gowned up and keen to get all the experience that the MIT could offer. Jack caught the familiar, antiseptic smell that always stuck in his throat, leaving a bitter aftertaste of something nasty, like corked claret.

'No surprises,' announced Dr Hardacre. 'Very little for a pathologist to work on, in fact.'

'Not really a difficult job then, doc.' As soon as he said it, Bugsy knew it was a mistake.

'No, Sergeant Malone. Nothing to it. When charred remains are not totally destroyed, all I'm expected to determine is the identity of the victim and the presence or absence of essential signs that could indicate whether the deceased was alive or not when the fire broke out. Then there's the cause of death, any potential poisoning or intoxication such as carbon monoxide, alcohol or drugs, and the possibility of third-party intervention or criminal involvement. As I say, nothing to it at all. Sometimes, I wonder why they pay me.'

'Sorry, doc. Ignore me.'

'I try to, Sergeant, but in view of the amount of space you take up, it isn't easy.' She continued. 'Our fire-damaged friend here was unconscious but not dead when he was immolated. However, there isn't enough of him left to establish possible poison or intoxication. Added to which, if I'd found any pieces of evidence in the ashes of the shack, they might easily have belonged to the late owner. As for intervention or criminal involvement — some pillar of the community chucked petrol over everything and set fire to it, causing a sizeable explosion. I think we can take it that was the cause of death.'

'Why has he got his fists clenched like that, Doctor?' Williams was keen to learn as much as he could. 'Might he have been fighting with someone?'

'No, DC Williams, it's known as the "pugilistic attitude" — a heat-related contraction of the limbs resulting in a characteristic boxing stance. It was well documented in the reports of the Pompeii burn victims after the eruption of Vesuvius. It can also be observed in the final stages of cremation. The body appears to rise up and threaten you with its fists.'

Blimey, thought Bugsy. *I thought I was tough but I wouldn't want to watch someone being cremated.* He supposed it was all in the interests of science.

'With regard to his identity, you'll be pleased to learn, Inspector Dawes, that I was able to obtain some DNA from his thigh bone. It comes with a caveat that it could be compromised.'

'We'll go with that, Doctor. We need all the help we can get.'

* * *

Despite the warning that the DNA might not get results, the police database threw up a match. It belonged to one Vincent Edward Parker, aka 'Nosy' Parker, due to his shady activities as a private investigator.

'He's got more form than a Derby winner,' observed DC 'Mitch' Mitchell. 'Burglary, criminal damage, robbery, going equipped, theft, handling, actual bodily harm, grievous bodily harm, common assault — he's had a try at pretty much everything on the charge sheet. He's done a couple of longish stretches inside, too.'

'According to police records, he lived in Aldgate. What was he doing in a market stall in Kings Richington, late at night?' wondered Gemma.

'Snooping on some poor devil, I expect,' decided Bugsy. 'Maybe they caught him at it and decided to put a stop to him.'

'That means we're back to the question of whether our arsonist knew Parker was in there when he set the fire or whether it was just bad luck,' said Jack.

'Sounds like we'll be looking at whether it was murder or manslaughter as a result of an unlawful act, sir.'

'Yes, and it will be for the CPS to decide when we have all the facts, Aled. First we have to find out who did it.'

'How d'you want to play it, guv?' asked Bugsy.

'We'll start by turning over Parker's office in Aldgate. We need to know what his movements were prior to his demise. I'm hoping for photographs or files on a laptop.'

'We're looking for details of anyone who had a burning desire to get rid of him,' quipped Bugsy, to groans from the others.

'Let's hope he didn't store them on his phone,' said Aled. The fire crew had found it, melted and red hot in the heat of the fire.

* * *

The police car pulled up outside 23a Downside Road. To Bugsy's disappointment, the kebab shop didn't open until evening. The team walked around the corner and Jack pushed open the side door.

'You can tell what kind of private investigator he was from his smart premises,' observed Gemma, avoiding the peeling, green paint. She wrinkled her nose at the stale smell that hit them as they went inside.

Jack led the team up the dingy stairs but when Bugsy trooped up after them, the stairs had had enough and his foot went through the tread with a splintering crack.

'Bugger!' he muttered, hopping about, trying to get his foot out without his bulk propelling him backwards down the stairs. He pulled his foot free but left his shoe behind. He eventually wrenched it out but minus the sole, which had been threatening to part company with the upper. for some time. He watched it fall through into the kebab shop below.

Meanwhile, at the top of the stairs, Jack had found the handwritten sign with the arrow pointing across the landing to the door. It was locked. Aled put his shoulder to it and it gave way without a fight. A brief search revealed that Parker had lived in a poky bedsit at the rear of the office. Aled and Gemma went through the pockets of his clothes in the wardrobe, crawled under the bed and lifted up the mattress. Finally, they searched in his kitchen cupboards and the fridge-freezer, which is where petty criminals quite often hid illicit cash. They found nothing to explain why he was in Kings Richington, nor what he was working on.

Parker's office revealed little more. Jack sifted through the detritus on his desk — several unpaid bills, a summons compelling him to appear before the local magistrate and a mouldy ham sandwich. The filing cabinet contained long-dead investigations of no relevance and a half-empty bottle of whisky. The wastepaper bin, often a source of useful intelligence, was full of parking tickets.

Aled and Gemma emerged from the smelly bedsit.

'Anything?' asked Jack.

Aled shook his head. ''Fraid not, sir. A bag of dirty washing destined for the launderette and a crate of empty bottles.'

'Where's his laptop?' Gemma looked around. 'The power cable's still plugged in the wall, so he must have one. That'll be where the records are kept.'

'Well, he didn't have it with him when he died.' Aled recalled.

Bugsy appeared in the doorway. 'It'll be in his car.'

'Good of you to join us, Sergeant,' said Jack.

'Sorry, guv. I put my foot through the stairs. Couldn't get my shoe out.'

'Do we know anything about his car?' asked Jack.

'We do now.' Bugsy picked up the summons. 'It's an old blue Volvo hatchback. He was summonsed for bald tyres. This has got a description and the registration number.'

'Well done, Sarge,' said Gemma. 'I wonder where it is now?'

'Parked in Kings Richington somewhere. It'll have his laptop and camera in the boot — standard kit for a private dick. I'll get Norman Parsloe's lads to look for it.'

Not for the first time, Jack was reminded what a top copper Bugsy was. Two minutes and he'd cracked it — while wearing only one shoe.

* * *

It didn't take long to track down Parker's car. It was still parked where he'd left it — less than a hundred yards from Jericho's shack. As Bugsy had predicted, his laptop and camera were in the boot. Unsurprisingly, the laptop was password protected. As Bugsy pointed out, in Nosy Parker's line of business, information was money and you couldn't risk anyone else having access to it, not unless they'd paid for it first.

It took Clive, the MIT techie, no more than fifteen minutes to hack in. The team stood around him as he opened a list of folders. They were labelled with the names of clients who had hired his services, which was useful. Clive scrolled through.

'Stop there,' said Bugsy. 'We recognize that name, don't we, guv?'

'Right,' agreed Jack. 'Ludovic de Coleville owns the Coleville Gallery, down the posh end of Kings Richington.

Sergeant Malone and I had the dubious privilege of providing backup for Detective Inspector Banerjee's team when they searched for forgeries. The tip-off had been a good one, according to Ash, but they didn't find anything. I wonder what Mr de Coleville wanted with a private investigator? Can you open that folder, Clive?'

The first photographs were of a man and a woman in a hotel lobby. The man was signing the register. The next set showed them kissing, as they got into the lift together.

'Pretty obvious it's a divorce obbo,' said Bugsy. 'The woman is Mrs de Coleville. Cracking looker. I wonder who the lucky bloke is.'

Clive scrolled until he found Parker's report. 'He's David Wilson. His address is in Kings Richington, where he lives with his wife and mother. There isn't much else about him. I guess that's all you need, if you want to cite him in a divorce.'

Gemma was puzzled. 'I don't understand why de Coleville did all that sordid, last-century muck-raking. New divorce legislation puts an end to the blame game. Basically, the sole ground now is the irretrievable breakdown of the marriage. You can even apply online. Get the whole thing done and dusted in six months.'

'You seem to know a lot about it, young Gemma,' said Bugsy.

She nodded. 'I studied law before I joined the police. I keep my eye in. It comes in useful.'

'Given that de Coleville is nobody's fool and the Art Fraud lads think he's a crook, maybe he wanted to keep tabs on his wife for another reason,' suggested Jack.

'I don't see a motive here for de Coleville wanting Parker dead, though.' Williams frowned. 'More likely it would be the other bloke, Wilson, who wanted him out of the way. Perhaps he was scared his wife would find out. Parker could have been blackmailing him, he's the sort that would have seen a fast buck in it.'

'So far, we have two candidates for our arsonist-cum-potential murderer. Can someone cross-check their names against the credit card receipts from Corrie's Kitchen? If one of them was in there the night the blowtorch was stolen, that pushes them up the list.'

Clive tapped the names into the spreadsheet he'd made of the customers. He swivelled round in his chair. 'Sorry, sir. They both were.'

'Well, that's it, then.' Jack reached for his jacket. 'Come on, everyone, we'll call it a day and go to the pub. We've lots of interviews to do tomorrow. First round's on Sergeant Malone.'

'Just a minute, sir.' Clive was still scrolling through Parker's laptop. 'I've found some more photos in a different file, labelled "deal." The team trooped back to look. The photos were a bit blurred, as if they'd been taken through a dirty car window, but they were clear enough to see Ludovic de Coleville breaking into Jericho's shack and transferring something from his car. It was covered in a sheet.

'Clive, can you get a date and time when those pics were taken?' asked Jack.

'It'll be in the metadata. Give me a minute, sir.' He tapped away, then turned his screen, so that Dawes could see it.

Jack consulted his pocket book. 'The photographs were taken after Ash's first visit to the Coleville Gallery but before he returned with the search warrant. What does that tell us, guys?'

'He stashed fake pictures in the shack while Detective Inspector Banerjee was gone,' offered Aled.

'Then he went back later to set fire to them,' finished Gemma.

'Sergeant Malone, I think you and I need to have a few words with Mr de Coleville. We'll go nice and early in the morning.'

CHAPTER FOURTEEN

Ludovic de Coleville had regained his hubris, confident that the police had nothing on him. The forgeries were safely burned beyond recognition and he assumed, since he had heard nothing, that Rob Slater's heavies had silenced Parker. He didn't know the details and didn't want to. He was therefore unfazed when he found DI Dawes and DS Malone waiting outside the door at nine o'clock when he opened up the gallery.

'I'm sorry, I'm very busy this morning and I'm just on the way out to an important meeting. If you must waste my time, make an appointment with my wife for later in the week.' He moved towards the door but Bugsy blocked his way with his considerable and intimidating bulk.

'It doesn't work like that, Mr de Coleville,' said Jack. 'Either you answer our questions here or we take you down to the station. It's up to you.'

Sasha appeared from the kitchen at the back with two mugs of coffee. Ludovic dismissed her irritably. 'Not now, Sasha. Go away.'

'I'd prefer it if you stayed, Mrs de Coleville. We have some questions for you, too.' Bugsy produced prints of the photographs Parker had taken of Sasha and David Wilson, kissing in the hotel lift, and passed them to her.

She gasped in horror. 'Where did you get these?'

'They were stored on the laptop of a private investigator, hired by your husband,' replied Bugsy.

She turned on Ludovic. 'You've been having me followed? It was that odious little man with the greasy ponytail, wasn't it? How could you?'

Ludovic ignored her and spoke to Jack. 'Really, Inspector, I should have thought the police had better things to do with their time than interfere in private matters between a man and his wife. I'm a close personal friend of Commander Sir Barnaby and I shall certainly be making a complaint. Now, I'd be obliged if you would please leave.'

'We shall, Mr de Coleville. But first, would you like to give me your thoughts on these photographs?' Jack passed over several shots of him transferring some paintings from his Range Rover into the back of Jericho's shack. 'This is definitely you, isn't it?'

This time, Ludovic was clearly shaken. Despite the fact that he was all in black with his face covered and the photos didn't show the registration number of the car, he decided it would appear even more suspicious if he denied it. He recovered quickly. 'So what? The gallery store-room had become overfull with works of no consequence. I needed to store them somewhere, until I could pass them on to a lesser gallery that handles such items. I knew the shack was empty after the owner died, so I put them in there. Unfortunately, some vandals chose to burn it down before I could move the items on. I suggest the police would be better employed keeping the streets free of such hooligans, instead of harassing law-abiding citizens. Someone could have been badly hurt.'

Now for the killer blow, thought Bugsy. He glanced at Jack who was preparing to deliver it.

'Someone *was* badly hurt. There was someone inside the shack when the arsonist doused it in petrol and set fire to it. We have since identified the remains of that person as Vince Parker, the private investigator you hired to follow your wife.'

Sasha went white. 'Oh my God, Ludo. What have you done?'

'Shut up, you stupid woman!'

'Did you start that fire to get rid of Parker, Mr de Coleville?' asked Bugsy.

Ludovic hesitated before answering, considering the implications of anything he might say. 'Why would I do that, Sergeant? My business with the man was done. I'd paid him off and I didn't expect to hear from him again. I have no idea what he was doing in the shack. Possibly the vandals didn't know he was in there, either. Have you considered that?'

'If whoever torched it knew Parker was inside, that would be a murder charge. There's also a timing issue that we have to consider. Parker took these photos of you moving the paintings ten minutes after Detective Inspector Banerjee of the Art and Antiques Fraud Squad left your gallery to obtain a search warrant. That's something of a coincidence, don't you think?' Jack watched him closely. The man was starting to sweat, but only slightly.

'We're a suspicious lot, us coppers,' continued Bugsy. 'And we think Parker saw you hiding forged paintings and took those photographs in order to blackmail you. He was a nasty little weasel on a good day, with lots of previous for such crimes. We think you knocked him out, shoved his body inside the shack, doused it with petrol then set it alight with a blowtorch, that you'd pinched from a food outlet. What do you say to that?'

Ludovic set his jaw. 'Prove it.'

* * *

After they'd gone, Ludovic poured himself a treble whisky from the decanter he kept for important customers. What really worried him was that the coppers had got most of it right. Parker *had* been trying to blackmail him and he *had* wanted him out of the way, but the arrangement was that Slater would get rid of him. They also suspected that he'd set fire to the shack using the blowtorch he'd pinched when he picked up the food from Corrie's Kitchen. But he'd had no idea that Parker had been hiding in there at the time. What the hell was the man thinking? Why hadn't he shouted? The police seemed to think he'd been knocked unconscious. Looking on the positive side, Parker was out of the way now and even with the photos of the forgeries — now burned beyond recognition — they really didn't have any evidence that wasn't circumstantial. He just needed to hold his nerve, wait until the heat was off, then go and see Rob Slater. He'd been expecting to sell the forgeries to some dangerous blokes in the organized-crime racket. At least the police couldn't link him to that. He took a long swig of single malt and the warm glow braced him. It would be all right. They may suspect but the coppers couldn't prove a thing.

Sasha came out of the back room, white and trembling. 'You know about David and me,' she declared. 'Why haven't you said anything?'

He laughed mirthlessly. 'Well, to quote good old Rhett Butler, "Frankly, my dear, I don't give a damn." I just needed to know that your lover wasn't someone with brains, who could cause me trouble. Now I know it's Weedy Wilson, I'm not bothered.'

Sasha flushed with anger. 'I know more than you think, Ludo. I've listened when you've made phone calls, watched you load forgeries into the van to send to that gallery in the Barbican. Do you think I don't know that you're making big money?'

'In that case, why didn't you tell the police? Not that they would have believed you without any evidence. They'd merely have thought it was the mindless babbling of a bitter woman.'

'I didn't tell the police because I shall expect my share, and more, when I divorce you, you bastard—'

David's backhander knocked her to the ground and his signet ring slashed open her lip. 'Too late — I've already filed against you. And you'll be lucky to get the clothes you're standing up in, my darling.'

* * *

Back at the station, Jack and Bugsy were sharing what they'd learned with the rest of the team.

'I don't know about you, guv, but from the way he reacted, I don't think de Coleville knew Parker was in there when he torched the shack.' Bugsy had been up early and missed Iris's excellent breakfast, so he was satisfying a serious carb deficiency with a couple of sausage sandwiches and a doughnut from the canteen. 'I think he did it, but just to destroy the fake merchandise before Ash and his lads found it.'

'I agree,' said Jack. 'He looked shocked then guilty, but not of murder.'

'We haven't eliminated David Wilson from our enquiries yet, have we, sir?' DC Mitchell was a married man and if it was him having a bit on the side — which he wasn't — he wouldn't want some sleazy little private dick taking pictures. Whether he'd go as far as bumping him off was another matter, but experience told him some blokes might, in the heat of the moment.

'You're right, Mitch. But was he even aware that Parker was on their case? Perhaps we should give him a tug to see how much he knows.'

* * *

Now that the dead man had been identified and there were no grieving relatives to be informed, the *Richington Echo* ran a big, front-page article, with pictures of the burned-out shack. Unable to obtain any photographs of Parker, the reporter had contented herself with a quote from Chief Superintendent Garwood: *The deceased, Mr Vincent Parker, was well-known in the private investigation sector and no doubt his services will be missed by those who availed themselves of such.* Garwood had declined to comment on the fact that the deceased had also been well-known to the police and to HMPs Pentonville and Wormwood Scrubs. Nor had he commented on whether the police were treating it as murder, manslaughter or just a terrible accident. *Enquiries*, he'd said, *were ongoing but still at an early stage.*

'Look, Georgie.' Cynthia Garwood showed him the *Echo*. 'There's a picture of you in the market, standing on the charred remains of Jericho's shack.'

'Like a phoenix rising from the ashes,' proclaimed Garwood. 'Emerging from any catastrophe stronger, smarter and more powerful.'

'I was going to say like Guy Fawkes on Bonfire Night. Are you going to cut it out and paste it in your scrapbook?'

Garwood sighed. 'Cynthia, for the umpteenth time, it isn't a scrapbook, it's a record of my — oh, never mind.' He opened the paper to see if there was anything else of interest. 'There's a piece here about Jack Dawes's wife and the food poisoning incident, at your garden party. That won't be very good for business.'

'I know. I'd hoped that none of the ladies would speak to the press but obviously one of them did, to enjoy her five minutes of fame. It's really awful. Corrie is a great chef and a good friend. I still can't believe anything she cooked would have poisoned us but I didn't give them anything that she hadn't prepared . . . except . . .' She bit her lip. 'Oh, George. It couldn't have been, could it? I mean, you can't get food poisoning from something like that, can you? I think I should ring Corrie, just in case.' She went off like a two-quid rocket, leaving George with no idea what she was talking about.

* * *

Jack, Corrie and Carlene were in Coriander's Cuisine kitchen, reading the dreadful report in the *Richington Echo*. The article had been written by the paper's restaurant critic, who had acquired the job on the strength of a cookery GCSE and a fortnight's work experience at McDonald's. It may also have helped that she was the editor's niece. Her acquaintance with English grammar had been a passing one. She wrote exactly as she spoke, but in a rag such as the *Echo*, this went unnoticed. The article read:

Mrs Cynthia Garwood gave a tea party for ladies what raise money for, like, charities and that. Everyone puked. The grub was done by Coriander's Cuisine and there was cake and sarnies and random stuff. Nobody knows what made everyone throw up but it must of been dead nasty. There wasn't no one available at Coriander's Cuisine to comment, probably due to them being shafted by the food-poisoning police. One of the guests told the Echo's *reporter that she'd totally hurled her guts and deffo wouldn't be eating food from there, any time soon.*

'It's bad, Jack, and I don't just mean the grammar.' Corrie was worried. 'Business has dropped right off.'

'That's because everyone thinks we've been closed down, which we haven't,' said Carlene.

'It's not as damning as it might have been, Corrie.' Jack was searching for some crumbs of comfort. 'Look on the bright side. If it had been written by one of those sarcastic, up themselves, foodie journalists who write for the nationals, they'd have made a proper meal of it.'

Corrie's face was deadpan. 'This isn't funny, Jack.'

'Sorry. Slipped out.'

'People are bound to be wary, once an accusation of food poisoning has been made,' said Corrie. 'Chez Carlene is still doing well, though. Fortunately, it isn't generally regarded as having any connection with Coriander's Cuisine, it's more associated with Antoine's family and Le Canard Bleu.'

'It'll be OK, Mrs D.' Carlene put an arm around her. 'People will soon forget and you're still getting orders from your regulars. We haven't had to lay anybody off.'

'If only we knew what had caused it. Didn't you and Bugsy find anything, when you went to see Cynthia?'

'Sadly no,' said Jack. 'Mrs Garwood was adamant that none of the guests ate anything other than your food. She'd chucked the leftovers in the bin which had been collected by the council, so we couldn't take any samples to test. I'm not sure what more we can do.'

Corrie's mobile rang. She looked at the number. 'Speak of the devil.' She pressed the answer key. 'Hello, Cynthia. How are you?'

'I'm fine. No after-effects at all. Listen, Corrie. Remember when you asked if the girls had eaten anything other than the food you provided, and I said no? Well, I've been thinking about it. I don't know if it's anything — I can't think it would be — but I thought I should mention it. After all, it could be important, couldn't it?'

'Cynthia, spit it out for goodness' sake.'

'Jam. I gave them extra jam. You see, they'd finished all the raspberry you provided, to go with the scones and cream, so I got a jar of strawberry from my cupboard and put dollops of it in pretty little jam dishes — one on each table. They were a wedding present from George's Auntie Ethel. The jam dishes I mean, not the tables.'

'Thanks for letting me know, Cynthia, but I don't think you can get food poisoning from jam. Where did you buy it?' Corrie knew better than to ask if Cynthia had made it herself.

'I got it from the Ladies' Guild stall on the market. Their produce is always excellent. There was no mould on the top or anything like that.'

After the call had ended, Corrie shared the information about the jam with Jack and Carlene.

'We did a module on "safe homemade eating" at college,' said Carlene. 'The high sugar content of fruit jam adds an extra measure of safety and a barrier to decomposition. Low-acid vegetables, however, are higher risk foods and if they're not processed properly, they could cause botulism, which is potentially deadly.'

'Thanks, Carlene,' said Corrie. 'I'm not sure if that makes me feel better or worse, but I'm glad the cost of sending you to college wasn't wasted.'

'Honestly, darling, even without the benefit of Carlene's module, I don't think it could have been jam that made all those women sick,' said Jack.

'Neither do I. We're back to square one.'

CHAPTER FIFTEEN

When Fenella Wilson opened her front door at eight o'clock in the evening, she found two men on the step, holding up police warrant cards. Her stomach lurched. *This is it*, she thought. *They've found out that Jude and I poisoned Jericho and that I tried to poison Ida. They've come to arrest me.* It was her recurring nightmare come true.

'Mrs Wilson?' asked DI Dawes. 'Is your husband at home? We'd like a few words with him, if possible.'

She began to breathe again. What did the police want with David? 'Yes, of course. Please come in. He's in the drawing room with my mother-in-law.' She showed them in to where David and Ida were watching one of her mindless quiz programmes. 'David, these police officers want to talk to you.' She moved to switch off the television.

'I'm watching that!' protested Ida. 'Get out of the way, Fenella — go and make the officers some tea. Where are your manners?'

'Perhaps we could speak somewhere in private, Mr Wilson?' suggested Malone.

David stood up. He thrust his jaw forward belligerently. 'Why? There's nothing I shouldn't want my mother to hear. What's it about?'

'It's about a recent visit you made to the Richington Arms Hotel, sir.' Bugsy was gratified to see Wilson's expression change from stroppy to scared. *That's put the wind up him.*

'I see. Please come into the dining room.'

'Would you like some tea?' asked Fenella, curious to find out what it was about.

'No, thank you, madam. We're fine.' *At present*, thought Jack, *it wasn't their job to tell Wilson's wife he was having an affair. That could change, if he was subsequently charged with something.* They sat down at the dining table and Bugsy produced the photographs that Parker had taken of Wilson and Sasha de Coleville, signing the register and kissing in the lift.

'Could you please confirm that this is you and Mrs de Coleville, sir?' asked Bugsy.

Wilson flushed guiltily, like a small boy caught filching biscuits from a tin. 'You know it is. I don't see what it has to do with the police. Adultery isn't against the law, the last time I checked. Where did you get these photographs? It's an invasion of my privacy.'

'No, sir, adultery isn't a criminal offence. But murder is,' said Jack. 'These photographs were taken by a private investigator called Vince Parker. He was hired by Mrs de Coleville's husband. If you read the report in the *Echo*, you will be aware that Parker was burned to death in a market stall. The arsonist used petrol and a blowtorch, which was stolen from a fast-food outlet called Corrie's Kitchen. We have evidence that you were in there the night it disappeared. Can you explain any of that, sir?'

'I can explain why I was out buying food. It was for my mother. My wife had cooked chicken for supper and Mother didn't fancy it. She wanted Italian food but my wife wouldn't make it for her, so I went out and bought some. They do a particular good Steak Ragu Pappardelle in Corrie's Kitchen, but I didn't steal anything. I can't explain the rest of what you've told me. I had no idea Ludovic de Coleville was having us spied upon and I'm sure Sasha hadn't either. I can't say I'm surprised. He was always a bully and a sneak at school. It seems he hasn't changed. But I can assure you, I had nothing at all to do with the death of that man, Parker.'

'Did he try to blackmail you, Mr Wilson? Threaten to tell your wife? It would be a motive for getting rid of him, wouldn't it?' asked Bugsy.

'Definitely not. I keep telling you, I've never met the man.'

Fenella, in the kitchen, with her ear pressed against the doors of the serving hatch, had heard all she needed to know. Ida had put him up to this. She had always wanted her son to marry that woman, Sasha — all blonde hair and simpering submissiveness. All the same, Fenella didn't believe David could kill anyone — he didn't have the balls. She was aware of the irony and almost laughed out loud.

David showed the police officers out and returned to the drawing room where Ida was watching a soap and Fenella was reading the *Echo*. The article about the food poisoning was sketchy to say the least, but she guessed that was where her jam must have ended up — at a posh garden party. At least nobody had died this time.

'What did the police want, David?' she asked innocently.

'Nothing that need concern you,' he replied. 'I reported that my wallet had been stolen in the Richington Arms Hotel. I was meeting a business colleague there. They came to take a statement.'

'A detective inspector and a detective sergeant — goodness me,' declared Fenella. 'The police *must* have time on their hands.'

'Why shouldn't they send senior officers?' snapped Ida. 'My son is an important man. You'd do well to remember that, Fenella.'

Watching Ida slurp down a second schooner of dark brown, syrupy cream sherry, Fenella saw an even better means of administering the antifreeze. She needed to talk to Jude.

* * *

'What d'you reckon, Bugsy?' The two police officers were having a swift half in their local on the way home. 'Did Wilson do away with Nosy Parker?'

Bugsy emerged from the depths of his ale with a foam moustache. 'Nah. My money's on de Coleville and I don't buy his story about some random vandals setting the fire. He's a nasty piece of work. Banerjee reckons he's involved with some serious goons. I bet he wouldn't think twice about topping somebody if he thought his forgery racket was under threat.'

'You don't think Parker was blackmailing Wilson? He looked worried when he thought his wife might find out he was playing away.'

'I reckon it's his mother he's scared of. Did you see her? Face like a bag of spanners. She'd frighten me.'

Jack grinned. 'I agree. I think he was telling the truth when he said he didn't know he and his lady friend were being watched. It has to have been de Coleville, but like he said, we have to prove it. And so far, we haven't much to go on.'

'We'll get him, Jack, we always do. We're the dynamic duo of the MIT.'

Jack rolled his eyes. 'Bugsy, do you know we've been in here for over half an hour and you haven't bought any food? You're not sickening for something, are you?'

'Iris is cooking beef stew and dumplings for supper. Don't want to ruin my appetite, do I?'

CHAPTER SIXTEEN

Fenella was trying to hold a conversation with Judith while she was underneath a Ford Focus, fixing the exhaust. It wasn't easy.

'Did you read in the *Echo* about that garden party where all the guests were sick, Jude?'

'Yep.'

'Do you know what caused it?'

'Nope.'

'I think it was my jam with the ethylene glycol in it.'

Jude slid out from beneath the car. 'You don't know that. It might just have been food poisoning, like the paper said. And anyway, how would your jam have got there? It said the food was professionally catered.'

'The party was at Mrs Garwood's house. She's the wife of Chief Superintendent Garwood. She often buys produce from our stall, doesn't she? You've served her yourself.'

'That doesn't mean she bought your jam. And how would one jar have made them *all* sick?'

'Well, as none of them was seriously ill, I'm guessing they each ate a small amount — maybe in a slice of sponge cake or on a scone.'

'It's possible, I suppose. But there's no way it can be traced back to you. They believe it's food poisoning and even a non-cook like me knows, you don't normally get that from jam. It's usually stuff like chicken or shellfish.'

'Jude, I've gone too far to give up now. I've found out David is having an affair.'

Judith guffawed. 'Your David — mummy's boy — having naughties on the side? Who with, for goodness' sake?'

'Sasha de Coleville.'

Judith guffawed even louder. 'Christ, Fen, she's been round the block so many times, she's almost screwed herself into the ground. And the woman has the IQ of a deckchair.'

'I know — and a figure like an anorexic stick insect — all thigh gap and collar bones. But Ida always wanted David to marry her. He was even engaged to her once. I'm sure the wicked old bat has been egging him on. I need more of the ethylene stuff, Jude. I'm going to put half a pint of it in her sweet sherry. That should see her off. She's the only one who drinks it, so nobody else will get hurt this time.'

'OK, but be bloody careful. Don't take any chances, such as going out and leaving her with it, like last time. Stay and make sure she drinks it. When does she normally have sherry?'

'Any time she feels like it, but mostly in the evening, before dinner. She'll have at least a couple of those big schooner glasses — says it aids her delicate stomach. Delicate, my arse. She's got a digestive system like an industrial macerator. I'll do it while David's out with that woman. He always turns his phone off, so he won't know about it until it's too late. That'll make him feel really guilty — out tom-catting, while his poor mother's having a heart attack.'

'Don't do anything daft, like calling an ambulance. Wait until you're sure she's carked it before you ring anybody.' Judith fetched a container of the antifreeze. 'This stuff is neat, totally undiluted, no colour, no smell and it hasn't been embittered, so be careful.'

Fenella read the label which bore a black cross, with the warning, *Danger. Harmful if swallowed. Keep out of the reach of children.* She giggled. 'It doesn't say, "Keep out of the reach of malicious, foul old harridans who make your life hell."'

'What shall we put it in?' said Judith. 'You can't take it home like this.'

Fenella produced a half-empty sherry bottle from her shopping bag. 'Pour some in here. This is a new bottle I bought today. I poured half of it away to make room. No, don't touch it. It mustn't have your prints on it, just in case something goes wrong. Tonight, after David has left for his dirty weekend, I'll swap it for the one in the drinks cabinet.'

Judith nodded approval. 'That's better, Fen. You're thinking it through now.'

* * *

'You haven't forgotten I'm away again this weekend, Fenella?' David was in his bedroom, packing a case. She noticed he'd bought new thong underpants in a leopard print design, to replace the baggy, grey boxers he usually wore. He tucked them away hastily. 'It's one of those silly, corporate team-building exercises. Waste of time, in my opinion, but the CEO likes everyone to attend, so I have to go.'

'Yes, dear, I understand. Of course you must go.' Fenella was trying hard to keep calm, although she was shaking inside. This was her opportunity to change her miserable existence for ever. 'Do you know where you'll be staying?'

'Not yet. We're all meeting at an arranged point in the city. The people running the event will tell us when we get there. I shan't be able to call you. They take our phones away. It's part of the initiative test.'

You have to hand it to him, thought Fenella. *The bastard has got every angle covered.* 'Don't worry, dear. Your mother and I will be fine.'

'Try not to upset her, Fenella. She's an elderly lady and her heart isn't strong.'

'I shan't upset her.' *Not for long, anyway. It'll be over before she knows what's hit her.* 'Off you go and enjoy yourself.' *If bouncing up and down on that skinny, witless Barbie doll is your idea of a good time.*

Half an hour later, David gave Fenella and his mother a swift peck on the cheek. 'See you on Sunday evening, girls. Take care of each other.' He grabbed his keys and hurried out.

Look at him, the idiot, thought Fenella, watching him walk to his car with a spring in his step. *Does he really believe I'm so stupid that I don't know what he's up to? He won't be so full of himself when he gets home and finds his precious mother's dead.*

Ida called to her from the foot of the stairs. 'Fenella, I'm going up for my shower now and I'll want a decent meal when I come down.'

Fenella didn't answer.

'Fenella! Can you hear me? I'd like lamb cutlets with mint sauce, baby carrots and mashed potatoes. Proper mash — not that disgusting, lumpy sludge you usually dish up. Do it properly, in the ricer.' She shouted down from the landing. 'Be assured, I shall tell David when he gets home if I'm not satisfied.'

'Oh no you won't,' muttered Fenella, under her breath. *You won't be telling tales to David, ever again,* she thought. *And I'm planning to tell you a few home truths, when you're breathing your last. Be assured of that!*

With Ida out of the way, she fetched the bottle of poisoned sherry from her car. Cautiously, she swapped it for the harmless bottle in the drinks cabinet, taking care not to get them mixed up. She hid the good stuff outside, in the Ladies' Guild store cupboard. She would swap them back again when it was all over.

* * *

It was over an hour before Ida reappeared, draped in a peach silk nightdress and negligée — another extravagant present from David. She'd been pampering herself, enjoying the thought that Fenella was slaving away in the kitchen preparing her meal.

In fact, Fenella hadn't been doing anything of the sort. While Ida was in the shower, she'd been sitting at the kitchen table, sipping a large cognac and rehearsing every detail of how she was going to kill her mother-in-law. This time, it wouldn't go wrong.

'Are my cutlets ready yet? You've had plenty of time, even at the speed you cook.' Ida sat down in her special armchair in front of the television and switched on a tedious quiz programme. The contestants were 'celebrities' and, in Ida's view, famous only for their spectacular lack of general knowledge.

'Not quite, Ida. Won't be long. Would you like a nice glass of sherry before you eat, dear?'

'Yes, I may as well. Goodness knows how long it'll be before I get any food, and I doubt it'll be edible, even then.'

This is it, thought Fenella. It was what Jude would have called a 'shit or bust moment'. She filled one of the large sherry schooners that she and David had brought back from Spain last summer. He had insisted they take his mother with them. It had been the holiday from hell. The glass held a full, ten fluid ounces.

'Here you are, dear.' *Get that down your scrawny neck.*

Ida took a slurp. 'This is nice and sweet. Is it the one David usually buys me?' She took another long glug, half emptying the glass.

'No, Ida, this is one I bought — especially for you. Drink it up and I'll pour you another.'

Fenella wasn't keeping track of time but it seemed like hours before Ida complained of feeling drunk.

'Goodness me, Fenella, this sherry is very strong. Did you buy it cheap, from the market? I feel quite tipsy.'

'Let me refill your glass.'

Ten minutes passed.

'Can't see screen properly.' Ida's speech was slurred. 'Can't hear quiz. Don't know what they're saying.' She pulled off her spectacles and dropped them on the floor. 'Fenella, I can feel my heart racing. Need my pills. Get them for me.'

In the planning of the deed, Fenella had wondered whether, when she reached this point, she would be overcome with remorse. Whether she would pull back from the deadly finale and summon help. Then she remembered the years of criticism, the orders issued without a please or thank you, the accusations that she was stupid, lazy, not good enough for her saintly son. Running to him with tales, so he would take her part and put Fenella in her place. Did she feel any remorse? Absolutely not!

Ida tried to stand but Fenella pushed her back down and thrust her face close, to make sure she heard every word. 'Did you know that David is having an affair with Sasha de Coleville — the girl you think he should have married?'

Ida nodded, drooling now. 'Lovely girl. Proper wife. Give me grandkids.'

Fenella laughed nastily. 'Oh no, she won't, you stupid old crone. Your precious David is sterile. No sperm in his balls, Ida, and it's your fault.'

Ida shook her head, violently. 'No. No.' She tried to push Fenella away, but her arms had become heavy and uncoordinated.

'Do you remember when he had mumps and you wouldn't have him treated? That's what caused it. You're the reason you never had grandchildren — and thank God for that. What a ghastly old granny you'd have been.'

Ida tried to get up again, a look of horror on her distorted face. 'Feel sick.' She threw up down her silk negligée and over her chair.

No problem with that, thought Fenella. *People having a heart attack often do vomit at some point, and it doesn't smell of antifreeze, only sherry.*

Ida was hyperventilating now, gasping for breath. 'Need pills. Heart. Help . . . dying . . .'

'That's right, Ida, you're dying. I put poison in your sherry.' She looked down, alerted by a stink. 'Oh dear, what a shame. You've soiled yourself. It's all over the expensive negligée that your beloved David bought you.'

'Can't breathe. Get help.' She clawed helplessly at her throat.

'No point,' said Fenella, calmly. 'You don't have long now — have you any last words?'

Her eyes widened with fear. 'Wicked. Wicked—'

'Don't waste your last breath cursing me. However much you think you hate me, it doesn't come anywhere near to how much I have despised you, my entire married life.'

Ida grabbed at Fenella's arm with a last jerky convulsion, then sank back onto the chair. Her eyes were still open. Fenella felt for a pulse, then closed them. It was done.

Half an hour later, during which time she cooked the lamb cutlets and mash, Fenella phoned for an ambulance. 'Please, come quickly. I think my mother-in-law has had a heart attack. No, I didn't see it happen, I was in the kitchen, cooking her supper.' She thought she sounded very convincing and so did the paramedics. They were very kind and sympathetic. They tried resuscitation but said it was too late. Cause of death was clear and as she was being treated for heart problems by Dr Griffin, he would be able to sign the death certificate. They were sorry for her loss but there was nothing she could have done.

After the body had been taken away, Fenella emptied the poisoned sherry bottle down the sink, washed it out several times and put it outside in the glass recycling bin, alongside several similar ones. She washed the schooner, retrieved the bottle of good sherry from the Ladies' Guild store cupboard, and put them both back in the drinks cabinet. Then she dragged the soiled armchair — Ida's special armchair — outside onto the patio. She would have it taken away as soon as possible and replace it with a bright, new one. It was an appropriate metaphor for her bright, new life. Satisfied that everything was in order, she phoned Judith.

'The old cow's dead, Jude. I've done it. They've taken her stinking, loathsome, putrid corpse away.'

'Right, Fen, now you need to ring David. I know his phone will be turned off but do it anyway. You believe he's on a business trip, don't forget. Keep calling him and leave messages. Remember, you're upset and need to tell him about his poor mother. It'll look suspicious if you don't try.'

'Good thinking. I'll do it straight away.

'Are you OK, Fen?'

'Couldn't be better.'

CHAPTER SEVENTEEN

The following morning, Fenella turned up at the market as usual, ready for her stint on the Ladies' Guild stall. News of Ida Wilson's death had travelled fast. This was mainly due to the bridge ladies of Laburnum Lodge, who never skipped a Saturday morning at the market, for fear of missing a bargain. They had heard of her demise from one of the care assistants, whose father happened to be the paramedic that had attended Ida the previous day.

Fortunately for Fenella, nobody seemed surprised or suspicious about Ida's death. She had consistently made such a fuss about her heart and often had mini "cardiac arrests" — particularly when she was losing at cards. As for Dr Griffin, although he hadn't expected her to die quite so soon, he conceded that it was entirely feasible, as heart problems could escalate very quickly. He would have no issues with signing the death certificate on the basis of the paramedics' assessment.

'I'm so sorry to hear about your mother-in-law, Mrs Wilson.' Beryl, from the vintage clothing stall, had come across to offer her condolences. She wore a bandana around her hair, a long skirt, a shawl and several rows of clinking glass beads. 'Your husband must be devastated. I understand he was very fond of his mother.'

'Yes, he was. I'm sure he'll be very upset when he finds out.'

Beryl looked surprised. 'Doesn't he know, then?'

'No, I haven't been able to contact him. He's away on a business trip, I haven't any idea where he is and his phone seems to be permanently switched off. I'm sure he'll ring home, when he can.'

'Oh, I see.' Beryl thought Fenella was taking it very well, especially having to manage the tragic death on her own. 'When you've sorted everything out, if you want to dispose of any of your mother-in-law's clothing, I'd be happy to take it off your hands. She always looked so smart.'

'Thank you. That's very kind.' Fenella knew Ida would be horrified to think of her clothes ending up on a vintage market stall, never mind 'common' people going about wearing them. She imagined Beryl in the fuchsia pink cape dress and stifled a giggle. She would parcel them up before David got back. If he had his way, no doubt he'd want to keep all his mother's things exactly as they were when she was alive. Well, she'd soon put a stop to that.

Fred the fishmonger came across, carrying a plastic bag. 'Didn't think you'd be here today, Mrs Wilson, what with your bereavement. Still, it doesn't do to mope at home, does it?' He held out the bag. 'Just some salmon and a few scallops. Got to keep your strength up.'

'Thank you so much, Fred. That's really kind. My mother-in-law always said how good your fish was. She so enjoyed it.' Fenella smiled to herself. *Cheap old scraps of fish off a market stall* was how Ida had described it.

Judith arrived, bringing coffee. 'I see the Richington gossip mill's gone into overdrive. I've had folk in the garage already, telling me the unhappy news about Ida. I tried to sound duly shocked and saddened. Have you heard from David yet?'

'Nope. I've left loads of tearful messages but he's obviously having such a good time, he's too weak to get out of bed and look at his phone. I'm so looking forward to giving him the sad news and a detailed description of how she died. Not the antifreeze part, obviously.'

'Obviously. Did she drink a lot of it?'

'Nearly half a pint. I've been in touch with the undertakers and it seems there's quite a backlog for cremations. She may have to stay in cold storage for a while.'

Judith suppressed a chuckle. 'Well, one thing's for sure — she won't freeze.'

* * *

'Oh, Sash, your poor mouth.' David kissed it, very gently. 'That man's a bully and a beast. He was just the same at school. All the younger boys were terrified of him.' *And so was I*, thought David, remembering the beatings.

Sasha snuggled up to him. 'Oh David, he had us followed by that horrid little man with the scruffy ponytail. I saw him at the bar in the Richington Arms Hotel. And now the man's dead — burned in Jericho's shack at the end of the market. The police came and questioned Ludo. They think he did it.'

'It wouldn't surprise me. The man's capable of anything. It's a pity they didn't arrest him, then and there, before he could hurt you.'

'Of course, he denied everything. What really worried him was that they had photos of him hiding some forged canvases. I don't know everything about his shady business but I know he makes a lot of cash from it.'

'The police came and questioned me, too. They thought I'd stolen the blowtorch and started the fire, to stop Parker from telling Fenella about us.'

'But you didn't, did you, darling?'

'No, of course not. Fenella doesn't suspect a thing, and even if she did, I doubt she'd do anything. We haven't slept together for years. She'd rather spend time with her butch

104

friend from the garage. Some days, it's all I can do to make her stay at home and look after Mother. The police didn't tell her anything and I can't imagine Ludovic would want it made public that his wife is cheating on him. Now Parker's dead, we can go on seeing each other without worrying.'

'But I'm going to divorce Ludo and you'll divorce Fenella so we can get married and have children. You want that too, don't you, David?'

'Of course I do, Sasha my angel, but don't let's do anything hasty. Mother and I live in Fenella's house and you live in Ludovic's pretentious monstrosity on the river. I expect the gallery's in his name, too. We need to find out what our legal positions are, before we burn our boats.'

She wrapped her arms around him and her hair cascaded over his bare chest, perfumed and golden. 'I don't care if we have to give up everything, as long as we can be together.'

His head on her shoulder, David's expression told a different story.

* * *

On Saturday evening, David and Sasha were dining at the riverside hotel and restaurant in Richmond. They sat outside at a table on the balcony, watching the swans on the Thames paddle serenely past. It was a balmy summer evening, perfect for romance.

'Isn't this wonderful, darling?' Sasha reached across the table and squeezed his hand. 'We've spent twenty-four whole hours alone together.'

'Absolute bliss, Sash,' said David, refraining from pointing out the oxymoron. Sasha was beautiful, sexy and affectionate but it had to be said, she was a few watts short of a lightbulb, even on her brighter days. With hindsight, it was probably the reason he'd broken off their engagement, believing he could do better. Then he'd married Fenella. What a mistake that had been. He should have listened to his mother.

'We must make the most of our freedom. We shan't be able to go out like this when we have babies.' She looked coy. 'We haven't been taking precautions, so it could happen quite soon.'

He wished she wouldn't keep talking about babies. This was not the time to tell her that children were out of the question.

'I suppose we could always ask your mother to babysit. Ida and I used to get on so well.'

David thought it was time to change the subject. 'Did you tell Ludovic how long you'd be gone, sweetheart? Has he phoned or messaged you?'

'No. I told you before. He doesn't care where I go as long as I keep working at the gallery when he wants me to. I thought he might ask when I was packing, but some man turned up in a van with a delivery — paintings, I think — and he just turned his back on me and hurried away. Something about this consignment being the big one.'

David didn't like the sound of that. Things were moving much too fast. He needed time to speak to his mother. 'I think I'll just pop up to our room and get my phone, darling. Just in case there are any messages for me. Look at the menu then order some wine, while I'm gone.'

Upstairs, he switched on his phone, which immediately flashed into life with dozens of missed calls and urgent messages — all from a frantic Fenella. Slowly, he scrolled through them with mounting horror.

The message late on Friday night read: *Please ring me the minute you get this.*

Ten minutes later: *You have to come home straight away.*

Then: *There's no way I can say this gently. Your mother had a cardiac arrest while I was cooking her dinner.*

And lastly: *There was nothing the paramedics could do. She's dead.*

The messages Fenella sent on Saturday morning were more practical. *I've made arrangements for her to be cremated as soon as the undertakers can fit her in.*

Followed by: *She was sick and doubly incontinent on her chair. It stinks so I've pushed it outside and arranged with the council to take it away.*

Finally: *How is the corporate team-building going?*

David imagined Fenella had enjoyed sending the messages.

He grabbed his bag and threw in his belongings, then took the stairs two at a time, not waiting for the lift. Down at the desk, he told the receptionist he had to leave in a hurry, due to a sudden family bereavement. He paid the bill then dashed out to his car, glad that he hadn't had time to drink any wine.

Seeing him rush through the lobby, Sasha ran after him. She was outside on the hotel steps when his car roared past.

'What about me?' she screamed, and burst into tears.

CHAPTER EIGHTEEN

It was early evening, towards the end of a hot summer's day. In the opulent Slater Gallery, the setting sun filtered through the blinds and glinted off green glass — a trio of conceptualist gin bottles, entitled *Anarchic Fusion*. The expensive decor had been designed to provide an ambience of quality and affluence, without tasteless ostentation. Lyrical cadences of Debussy's 'Clair de lune' floated down from discreet speakers, complementing a conceptualist acrylic painting of a moonlit sky. This was the painting of the month, displayed on an easel in the centre of the gallery.

The smart young receptionist, in her navy suit and crisp white blouse, was setting out drinks for cocktail hour visitors, as she did every evening at this time. The door chimes heralded customers. She turned, smiling, ready to welcome them. Three men sauntered in. She decided they were not the typical art lovers who usually frequented the Slater Gallery, or even the Barbican Centre, come to that. However, you couldn't judge by appearances. They'd probably turn out to be eccentric millionaires who chose to wear leather jackets and jeans at this time of day.

'Good evening, gentlemen. Are you looking for anything specific? May I offer you a drink?'

The last man in closed the door behind him and locked it. Then he turned the 'open' sign around to 'closed.' She became alarmed. All three were well-built and muscular, like bouncers outside a particularly seedy club. One of them casually picked up the gin bottles, one at a time, and hurled them at the wall.

She gasped. 'Please, stop! These items are valuable. I'm afraid all breakages will have to be paid for.'

They ignored that. 'We've come to speak to your boss. Is he here?' The foreign accent was strong but difficult to place.

'Well, yes, he's upstairs in the office, but I don't think . . .'

The ringleader took her by the shoulders and propelled her to a chair. 'You don't need to think, *dragă mea*. Sit down, be quiet and you won't get hurt.'

She watched, horrified, as the three men systematically took the showroom apart. They pulled down paintings and slashed them, threw ceramics to the floor and kicked over the easel bearing the prime exhibit.

'What the hell is going on here?' Rob Slater burst in, alerted by the racket of his gallery being wrecked. 'Stop that at once. Who are you? What do you want?'

'You know why we're here, Slater. We had a deal. We paid you much money for special goods. You didn't deliver. The boss doesn't like men who cheat on a deal. He thinks it's a double-cross.'

'No, it isn't, I can assure you.' Slater was starting to sweat. 'Please tell him, I haven't got the paintings. They were supposed to be delivered to me by my associate but the Art Fraud police were on to us and they had to be destroyed.'

'We don't believe you. Neither will the boss.' He turned to one of the heavies. 'Take the girl upstairs and keep her quiet.'

'Please, don't hurt her,' begged Slater. 'She doesn't know anything about the deliveries. She just runs the front of house and looks after visitors.'

'What sort of men do you think we are? We're not animals. We never hurt women, unless it's necessary. But double-dealing, cheating, clever bastards, who think they can swindle us and get away with it — that's another matter.'

The two goons closed in on Slater.

'No, please. I can explain. There's no need for violence, gentlemen. We can sort this out. I have some top-quality merchandise on the way, just give me more time—'

He was cut off by a blow, then another and another, until the bright lights of the gallery faded to black and his cries of protest dwindled to silence.

* * *

Detective Inspector Banerjee had several contacts in the Barbican Centre and news of the raid on the Slater Gallery reached him the day after it happened. Once again, he enlisted the help of MIT.

'We've had our suspicions about this gallery for some time, Jack. The word on the art grapevine is that it's the halfway house between the people who produce the forgeries and the organized-crime gangs who get their funding from it. Now, it seems, the owner has been badly beaten. He's in hospital in intensive care. Do you and Bugsy want to ride shotgun, while I find out what's been going on?'

'Yes, good idea. Are you thinking there could be a connection between Slater and de Coleville?'

Ash nodded. 'He was going to pass those fake paintings on to someone. Why not Slater?'

Bugsy nodded. 'Then you and your lads got too close and he had to burn the merchandise. Must've broken his heart.'

'And his bank account. My team have tried to trace the accounts of both Slater and de Coleville. Nothing out of the ordinary, so the real money must be going somewhere offshore. It's how organized-crime gangs operate.'

'Lucky buggers don't pay any tax,' observed Bugsy.

'I don't expect Slater feels particularly lucky right now.'

* * *

When Jack, Bugsy and Ash turned up outside the Slater Gallery, the young receptionist, not unreasonably, declined to open the door. After all, it could be a second coming from gangland. She pointed to the 'closed' sign, but after they held their warrants up to the glass, she let them in. 'I'm sorry but we've had a bit of trouble, as you can see.'

A bit of trouble? thought Bugsy. The place looked like a bomb had hit it. Fragments of glass and ceramics lay in an expensive heap where she had attempted to sweep them up. Paintings, slashed beyond repair, were stacked against the wall. He wondered what it would take for her to consider it a *lot* of trouble.

'Can you tell us what happened, miss?' Bugsy thought she had some bottle to still be there, after what must have been a frightening experience.

'I was getting ready for the usual influx of tourists that we get in the evenings at this time of year. They have an early dinner in their hotels, then come to the Barbican to look around. Mr Slater was upstairs in his office, doing the accounts. Suddenly, these three tough-looking men came in. Not at all the kind of customers we like to attract. They looked like thugs and as it turned out, that's exactly what they were.'

'Did they say what they wanted?' asked Ash.

'Not at first. I said to myself, "Don't be judgemental, Monica. They may be bona fide customers," so I offered them a drink. That was when one of them picked up *Anarchic Fusion* — three gin bottles — and threw them at the wall. Well, as you can imagine, I was a bit annoyed.'

'Of course you were, Monica,' comforted Bugsy. Jack could see her warming to him. Women always did, young and old. 'What happened then?'

'They asked if Mr Slater was in. I said yes, he was upstairs in his office but I didn't think he would see them, as he didn't want to be disturbed. That was when the really ugly one — face like a Notre-Dame gargoyle — told me I didn't need to think, just to sit down and be quiet.'

'Was that when they started to trash the place?' asked Ash.

She nodded. 'Mr Slater heard all the banging and crashing and came down to see what was happening. He was angry at first but then they said something about their boss not liking clever bastards who double-cross him and don't deliver what's been agreed. Mr Slater became cooperative, then. They really were very intimidating. Gargoyle told one of the others to take me upstairs and keep me quiet. Well, I was really scared. I didn't know what "keeping me quiet" involved. Mr Slater told them not to hurt me because I didn't know anything about any deliveries, which is true.'

'Did he hurt you, Monica, the bloke who took you upstairs?' asked Bugsy.

'No. He went into the staff kitchen, put the kettle on and made me a cup of tea. Then he asked where the CCTV equipment was and smashed it, so there wouldn't be anything on the video.'

'Could you hear what was going on in the gallery?'

'No, not really. There were lots of thumping noises and poor Mr Slater cried out a few times. Then it went quiet and Gargoyle shouted up to my thug, "Tie her up" — but he didn't. He told me to stay put, until they'd gone. Of course, when I did go down, I found Mr Slater unconscious and covered in blood. One of his legs was at a funny angle, so I guessed it was broken. I called an ambulance and the police.'

'Would you recognize these men again?' asked Banerjee.

'I could try, but one violent thug looks much like another, don't you find? They all had beards and tattoos and the ringleader was badly scarred, as if someone had slashed his face.'

Bugsy reached into his jacket pocket and pulled out a photograph. It had half a KitKat stuck to it. He peeled it off and smoothed out the photo. 'Monica, do you know this man?'

She looked at it and recognized him at once. 'Oh yes, that's Mr de Coleville. He's a frequent visitor. Such a charming man and very attractive. He and Mr Slater are in the same line of business. Mr de Coleville is very knowledgeable. I believe he has a rather nice gallery of his own, somewhere out of town. He sends some of his stock to Mr Slater occasionally, and Mr Slater sells it on.'

It was clear to all three coppers that Monica either knew nothing about Slater's nefarious deals, or she was an extremely convincing liar. They opted for the first.

'One last question, Monica,' said Bugsy. 'Does Mr Slater have a wife or partner?' He was thinking it might be necessary to contact next of kin, from what he'd just heard.

'Oh, no, not a wife, he's gay. I'm not sure about a partner. I don't think he has anyone special at present. But everyone likes him.'

'Clearly someone doesn't,' muttered Banerjee.

They went to the hospital to see if Slater was fit to be questioned, but the doctor said he was on life support. He'd been put into an induced coma and wouldn't be well enough any time soon — if at all.

'Nasty business,' said Jack, on the way back to Kings Richington. 'Looks like the bloke isn't going to make it.'

'Well, guv,' said Bugsy, 'if you're going to sup with the devil, you need a bloody long spoon.'

CHAPTER NINETEEN

When David Wilson arrived at his front door, he was shaking so much he couldn't find his key. All the way home, he'd hoped it had been a horrible hoax. Fenella's warped idea of a joke. He knew she resented his relationship with his mother but surely she wouldn't pretend Ida was dead simply to upset him. He supposed there was a slim chance she'd found out about Sasha. Maybe his mother had told her out of spite. Maybe the police had told her after all. If they had, he would certainly make a complaint. This could be Fenella's way of making him come home. Yes, that's what it would be. He'd go inside and find them both watching some quiz on TV. Then he spotted it, pushed out onto the drive. It was Ida's chair, soiled and covered in vomit.

While he was still rummaging in his pockets for keys, the front door suddenly opened and Fenella stood there, unemotional and resolute. 'You eventually picked up my messages, then?'

'Yes.' He pushed past her and strode into the drawing room, still half-hoping to see his mother watching TV, eager to make yet another, stinging complaint about his wife. 'What happened, Fenella? Mother was perfectly fine when I left. How could she have died so suddenly?'

'It was her heart. You know how she insisted her life hung by a thread? Well, the thread finally snapped.'

'Couldn't you help her? Call a doctor, or something?'

'I was in the kitchen, cooking her evening meal. I left her watching her favourite quiz programme on TV. When I came in to tell her the food was ready, I found her dead in her chair.'

'I don't know how you can be so pragmatic about it. She was such a lovely lady and a wonderful mother. I can't believe I'll never see her again. It's such a shock.' To Fenella's disgust, he began to blub. 'Poor Mummy. If I'd been here to look after you, you might still be alive.'

Almost certainly, thought Fenella, wryly. 'Never mind, David, I'm sure what you were doing was more important to you than your mother. Anyway, I've put her on the waiting list to be cremated. You can arrange the funeral later. I dare say all the old biddies at Laburnum Lodge will want to attend, if only for the sherry and the buffet afterwards. I thought we'd get Coriander's Cuisine to cater it. They're very good and I didn't believe that food poisoning scare in the press, not for a single minute. I'm quite sure it was down to something else entirely.'

'Fenella, please be quiet. Show some respect. If all you can do is witter on about funeral arrangements, I don't want to listen to you. I'm going upstairs to sit in Mother's room. I need some time alone, to grieve and take in this terrible tragedy.'

Fine, thought Fenella. *Off you go. You'll find it a bit different, though*. She had parcelled up Ida's clothes to give to Beryl on the clothing stall. The bed was stripped and she'd taken the curtains down to be cleaned. All the toiletries on the dressing table had gone in the bin and the various knick-knackery that cluttered Ida's room was in a box, destined for the charity shop. The whole exercise had been incredibly cathartic for Fenella. Obviously not for David. She could hear him blubbing even louder.

She poured herself a glass of Châteauneuf-du-Pape — the really good stuff David kept for special occasions — and contemplated her future. While she had been clearing Ida's room, she had found a copy of her will, hidden under the mattress. As expected, Ida had left all her money to David. What Fenella hadn't anticipated was that there would be so much of it. The old girl had been worth a fortune. If, as now seemed inevitable, she and David divorced, would she get half in the final settlement? Their relationship had deteriorated over the years, largely due to his mother living with them. His affair with Sasha de Coleville was the last nail in the coffin. She felt she deserved every penny of her share. Goodness knows, she'd earned it.

She poured another glass of wine and googled it. The law wasn't clear. It seemed the basic rule was that money inherited during a marriage became part of the 'marriage pot' to be divided on divorce. But it was far from cut and dried. It depended, apparently, on the needs of each party. She would speak to Judith about it.

When she eventually went upstairs to bed, having finished the bottle of wine, David had blubbed himself to sleep on Ida's unmade bed. She looked at him, tearstained and pathetic. His thinning, biscuit-coloured hair and sallow complexion reminded her of a shabby old Steiff bear. Whatever had she seen in him? Come to that, what did Sasha de Coleville see in him? Her husband, Ludovic, was dashingly handsome with thick, dark hair and a captivating smile. There was no accounting for taste.

* * *

The following morning, the atmosphere was decidedly frosty. David had spent half an hour locked in the bathroom, speaking earnestly on his mobile. Fenella assumed he was trying to build a few bridges with Sasha, whom he must have abandoned in something of a hurry. He had, in fact, been talking to his solicitor. He'd made an appointment to discuss his mother's will, that afternoon. As her sole executor, he intended to push probate through as quickly as possible and ensure that the money went into his personal account and not into the joint one.

'I shall be away most of the day, Fenella. There are important things I need to see to. I shall be speaking to the undertaker, fairly urgently. I won't allow Mother to be cremated. She always wanted to be buried next to my father.'

'But isn't he buried in a cemetery in Italy?'

'Yes. It was Mother's wish to be buried next to him when her time came. And as her only son, it's my duty to carry it out. I shall arrange to take her body over there as soon as possible. Incidentally, I shan't be coming back.'

'Are you expecting me to come with you?'

'Not at all. Now that I don't need you to look after my mother, we can go our separate ways. You have this house and your little job — and your butch motor mechanic.'

'And you have your mistress,' Fenella snapped. 'Is she going with you?'

David looked taken aback. It seemed she did know about his affair with Sasha. He ignored the question. It was none of her business. 'Of course, I shall resign from my job — I shan't be needing one. With Mother's money, I can buy a house in Italy as a base and travel abroad. It's what Mother always wanted for me.'

'I think my solicitor may have something to say about that, when it comes to the divorce settlement.'

He laughed unpleasantly. 'I shall be long-gone before any divorce takes place. Once I've got everything sorted, I'm off — and I shan't be leaving a forwarding address. Mother left *me* that money and she'd never rest in peace if she thought you could touch one penny of it.'

* * *

After his spiteful outburst, David hurried from the house to make arrangements for his mother's coffin to be flown to Rome. Then he went to see his solicitor to make absolutely sure that his inheritance would be available to him — and only him — as soon as possible. Despite the solicitor's advice, he didn't see the need to file for divorce or make a new will, as he intended to travel the world. If Fenella thought she had a claim on his money, she'd have to find him first.

Despite her initial elation at finally being Ida-less, Fenella was feeling angry and bitter. She was now convinced that David had married her not because he wanted her for his wife, but because he had wanted a carer for his mother. At the age of twenty-seven, he had clearly become disenchanted with having to do it himself. After fifteen long years of witnessing Fenella putting up with Ida's nasty sniping and criticizing, he was blithely planning to push off and leave her without a penny. She had no doubt that he had originally seen Sasha de Coleville as a suitable candidate for the carer's vacancy after he'd dumped her, his wife. She wondered if that would still be the case, now that he no longer had a mother to look after.

Fenella went to see Judith at the garage. They had an early and very large glass of wine while Fenella explained what had happened and David's imminent departure to Rome.

Judith was puzzled. 'Why was David's father buried in Italy?'

'Apparently, he and Ida had been on their honeymoon in Rome. She threw a coin in the Trevi Fountain, thinking it was just a few lire. Then she realized it was actually the equivalent of twenty quid. She made him jump in and get it back. He was quite a lot older than her and he had some sort of seizure. That's what she told David, anyway.'

Judith was dumbfounded. 'Why on earth would she do that?'

'Because she was a cheapskate. You don't get to be as rich as Ida by being generous. Even though she was going to inherit all her husband's considerable fortune and a massive house, she considered it too expensive to fly him home, so she left him behind, buried in a cemetery in Italy. David was born nine months later — the product of a honeymoon shag.'

'So it's always been just David and his mother?'

'Yep, for forty-two years. They've never been parted, as he never tired of telling me. When David and I got married, she even came on our honeymoon with us. Afterwards, I refused to go and live with him in his mother's house. I knew what it would be like if I was under her roof. I'd just be a skivvy, waiting on her. So reluctantly, he moved in with me. Scared she'd lose control over her precious baby boy, she sold up and persuaded him to let her live with us. I still became her skivvy, but in my own house. I'm not sure whether that was better or worse.'

Judith thought about it. 'He never really had a father, did he? That explains a lot.'

'I dare say a father would at least have had his son's balls sorted out when he had mumps as a teenager.'

Jude giggled. 'Sounds like his father didn't have much in the way of balls, either.'

'Maybe not, but at least he had enough to father a child. Trouble is, that child has never grown up.'

'What are you going to do, Fen? You can't let the bastard get away with this. That's fifteen years of your life that you'll never get back and nothing to show for it. No gratitude, no affection and no reward. I guess it's some consolation that they'll both be out of your life.'

'I've no idea what I'll do. I thought you might have some ideas.'

Judith opened another bottle. 'I know what I'd do.'

'What? I can't see how I can stop him.'

Judith poured Fenella another large glass. 'You can stop him the same way you put a stop to Ida — with ethylene glycol. If he dies before he can divorce you, all the money will come to you, as next of kin. Do you know if he's made a will?'

'Yes, he made one when we were first married. We both did, leaving everything to the surviving spouse.'

'Then we need to move fast, before he has a chance to change it. We can't use the heart attack ploy because he isn't under the doctor for anything, so you need to make it look like suicide. Overcome with grief at the death of his poor mother. Couldn't face life without her. Balance of the mind and all that.'

'Jude, do you really think we could get away with it? It would be wonderful. I could afford to stay in my house and you could come and live with me.'

'Of course we could. But we need to think it through, properly. Leave nothing to chance. We can't afford to make any mistakes.' She went quiet, thinking hard. 'Is there anything sweet that David eats or drinks every day, come rain or shine? Obviously, you'll have to be there to administer the poison, but I think it will be safer if you're out of the way as soon as you've done it, and definitely before they find him. I mean, what kind of man would top himself with his wife in the house? We've got to make this entirely plausible.'

Fenella drank more wine. 'No. It's no use. I can't think of anything sweet he has every day . . .' She stopped. 'Hang on, yes I can. Ovaltine.'

'Ovaltine?' Judith was amused.

'Yes. Every night before bed, he makes himself a mug, with full cream milk and loads of sugar. His mummy always made it for him, when he was little. Swears he couldn't possibly sleep without it. Over the years, it's become more of a tyranny, than a habit. If he goes away anywhere, he has to take some with him, in case the hotel doesn't have any. There was one occasion when they didn't, and he almost had a panic attack. Seriously, he was hyperventilating. He even insisted on it on our wedding night. I had to sit and watch him drink it before he'd come to bed.'

'Fen, that's like something out of a bad French farce. It would be funny if it wasn't pathetic. But it does give us an opportunity. How does this sound? One night, soon, round about his bedtime, you tell him he's looking tired. Say you understand how much he's missing his mother. You really don't mind about him going abroad to live. If you can bear to spit the words out, tell him you're sorry you reacted the way you did and you want to part as friends.'

'Jude, do I really have to say that?'

'Yes. You have to lull him into a false sense of security, so he won't suspect anything. Tell him to go and have a nice bath and hop into bed and you'll bring up his Ovaltine, then leave him to go to sleep. Just like his precious mummy would have done, when he was little. He'll go for it, trust me. Men are such clowns. They'll believe anything if it suits them.'

'OK, then what?'

'You make his Ovaltine with half a ton of sugar and a healthy dose of ethylene glycol. Or do I mean an unhealthy dose? Then, you leave him in bed to drink it and come straight here to me. I'll provide you with an alibi. We'll say that you and David had argued, he was very depressed and you needed company. You'd been with me all afternoon.'

'How do we make them believe he's committed suicide though?'

'Good question. Does David keep antifreeze in your garage?'

''Yes, there's a plastic container of it on the shelf.'

'I'm assuming it will have his fingerprints on it and not yours.'

'Oh, yes. He doesn't allow me anywhere near that precious Lexus his mother bought him. He does everything himself.'

'Good. You take that container, wearing gloves, obviously, and you empty it. I'm assuming it will be the safe stuff, not the highly toxic, like mine.'

'Almost certainly. He makes sure when buys it.'

'Right. Next, you replace the contents with the dangerous stuff that I'll provide and leave it in the kitchen, next to the tin of Ovaltine. It won't matter that your fingerprints will be on the mug and milk saucepan, as well as David's. You live there, so it would be strange if they weren't. I'm assuming that once he's drunk it, he'll experience the same symptoms as Ida — intoxication, confusion, palpitations and finally, heart failure. It works fast so they may find him dead in bed or on the bathroom floor, if he feels sick and makes it that far. You won't be there to see. Obviously, they'll do a post-mortem and the pathologist will find ethylene glycol in his blood. But they'd have to think of antifreeze poisoning in the first place, to decide to do the test. If someone turns up dead with non-specific symptoms, a pathologist wouldn't immediately think, "Oh, it must be antifreeze poisoning," unless they find a container of the stuff close by. We need to point them in the right direction.'

'What if he tries to phone for help, in the few moments before he loses his faculties?'

'Good point. Do you have a landline?'

'No, just mobiles. David keeps his in his briefcase when he's not using it, otherwise he forgets where he left it.'

'OK, so you take it out and put it somewhere he can't find it in a hurry. After a few minutes, he won't be in any fit state to look for it anyway. You can put it back afterwards'

'I'll put it in my knicker drawer.'

'Don't switch it off. It could look suspicious.'

'Jude, you're so clever. You could make a living out of this planning lark.'

'You're thinking of wedding planners, Fen. I don't think there's much call for murder planners. And I'm pretty certain it would be illegal, but thanks anyway.'

CHAPTER TWENTY

When Ludovic telephoned Rob Slater's gallery, Monica answered the phone and recognized the deep, honeyed tones immediately.

'Hello, Mr de Coleville. How can I help?' She was always pleased to hear from him — such a suave, charming man. He reminded her of a young George Clooney.

'May I speak to Rob, please?'

'No, I'm afraid he's in hospital. He's very ill — on life support, I understand. I thought the news might have reached you, as you're in the same line of business.'

Ludovic had a premonition of doom. 'Has he had some kind of accident?'

'I wouldn't call it an accident. Some thugs forced their way in and beat him up, badly. They smashed up the gallery, too. They've caused thousands of pounds worth of damage.'

Ludovic went cold. He was torn between two courses of action, to visit Rob in hospital or to stay well away. This was the work of the mob, flexing their considerable and far-reaching muscles. It could only have been because he hadn't been able to deliver the forged paintings. What would they do if they found out that he was the one who had burned them? Never mind that he had attracted the unwanted attention of the Art Fraud police. It didn't bear thinking about. He wondered how much Rob had told them when they were beating him up. Did they know that he, Ludovic, had another big consignment, ready to move? It was an important one, worth hundreds of thousands to the organization. He needed to ask Rob what he should do with it.

'I'm so sorry to hear that, Monica. I'll go along to the hospital and see how he is — take him some grapes.'

He switched off his phone before she had a chance to tell him to forget the grapes, as poor Mr Slater had had most of his teeth bashed in.

* * *

Ludovic found a parking space at the hospital after driving round for some time. Finding the intensive care unit was nearly as arduous. Finally, he asked a porter for directions.

'Who you looking for, squire?'

'Robert Slater. He was brought in a few days ago. I just need a quick word.'

'Oh, him.' The porter sucked his teeth, doubtfully. 'You a relative?'

'No, I'm a business colleague.'

'No chance, then. He's in a coma for a start and he's got coppers sitting either side of him, for when he comes out of it.'

Ludovic strode briskly away.

'Hang on a minute, mate!' the porter called. 'They might let you look at 'im through the glass.'

The presence of police officers was enough to persuade Ludovic that a fast exit was required. They would be waiting to hear anything Rob said, if he regained consciousness — but more likely, they were protecting him against a further attack. In either event, it was not a safe place to be. He found his car and drove back to the Coleville Gallery.

* * *

Back at the station, the team were reconsidering the extent of de Coleville's involvement in the art forgery racket and now his connection, if any, with Slater. How much did he know about Slater's beating? The man had claimed to know nothing about any illegal activities, but as DC Fox pointed out, he would say that, wouldn't he? Even if he was up to his neck in it.

Clive, who was tapping away on his computer, suddenly stopped and scrolled back. He called to Jack. 'Sir, have a look at this.' They gathered around Clive's desk. 'These are the files I hacked from Vince Parker's laptop. Look at this one.'

The folder was named 'Slater' and it contained details of the shady work Parker had done for him over the past couple of years. It seemed that Slater had needed a gun — not one that was purchased and licensed legally, but one that couldn't be traced back to him. Through his crooked, underworld contacts, Parker had obtained a Glock automatic handgun and a quantity of magazines, each holding thirteen rounds. The gun had come from Northern Ireland, with the serial number filed off. Parker had bought it for a meagre three hundred pounds and had sold it to Slater for a thousand.

'Well, now, I wonder why Slater wanted a gun,' said Jack. 'If it was to protect himself from the mob, it wasn't much use when he needed it. It was pretty cheap, although Parker made a big profit. Maybe it was faulty.'

'We can't ask him now, guv.' Bugsy put down the phone. 'That was the hospital. He just died.'

Jack sighed.

'But now we have a connection between Slater and de Coleville, apart from the frequent visits that Monica told us about,' observed Bugsy. 'They used the same private dick.'

'Slater probably recommended him,' said Aled.

'I think we should give de Coleville another tug,' suggested Jack. 'We'll ask him how well he knew Slater and did they have a working relationship. See if he lies.'

* * *

Already alarmed by Monica's account of Rob Slater's terrible beating, de Coleville was less than comforted by the presence of Dawes and Malone waiting outside the gallery when he returned. Reluctantly, he let them in.

'You're wasting your time, officers. I'm exercising my right to silence.'

'Well, don't exercise it too hard, Mr de Coleville,' said Bugsy. 'It isn't as robust as you might think.'

'Sergeant Malone's right,' agreed Jack. 'It would serve you better if you told us about your relationship with Rob Slater.'

Ludovic assumed a blank expression but was panicking inside. They may have started out as plods from an unspeakably limited gene pool, but they were getting dangerously close to finding out about his real business. He chose his words with care.

'Obviously, I've heard of the Slater Gallery. In the art world, we are all aware of other colleagues in the profession. But I wouldn't go so far as claiming Mr Slater and I had any kind of relationship.'

'How *would* you describe your dealings with him, sir?' Bugsy was scribbling in his notebook. It always unnerved villains because they could hardly ever remember what they'd said afterwards, but they knew it was all down in writing.

'I believe I've passed the time of day with him occasionally. Usually at fine-art auction houses or exhibitions of mutual interest. No more than that.' He knew Slater was in no condition to tell the police anything different.

Jack nodded to Bugsy who flicked back through his notes. 'Well, that's strange, sir, because we spoke to the young lady who runs the reception at the Slater Gallery, and she told us you were a regular visitor.'

Damn, thought Ludovic. He'd forgotten Monica. He should have warned her not to mention him to the police. It was obvious that they'd want to interview her. She may even have been there, when the raid took place. She hadn't said as much when he'd phoned, but then he hadn't given her the chance.

Bugsy continued. 'She also mentioned that you some-times provided stock for Mr Slater. What might that have been, sir?'

There was a long pause. 'I don't think I care to say any-thing more without my solicitor. So, unless you are going to arrest me, I'd like you to leave.'

Jack thought about it. They probably did have enough to arrest him, and hold him for questioning for forty-eight hours, but it was still mostly circumstantial. He thought, on balance, they'd find out more by letting him go and watching what he did.

'No, Mr de Coleville. You're free to go — for the moment.'

As they were nearly through the door, Bugsy did his 'Columbo' routine and turned back. 'Just one more thing, sir. You may not have heard but Mr Slater died of his injuries earlier today. You take care, now.'

* * *

Ludovic poured himself a large whisky. He knew he needed to get a grip and think clearly. He felt like he was trapped in a pincer movement — the police waiting to catch him out on one hand, and the mob waiting to break his legs on the other. Either way, he didn't fancy his chances. While he was ponder-ing his next course of action, his phone rang. It was Monica.

'I'm so sorry to bother you, Mr de Coleville, but I didn't know who else to contact. I dare say you've heard that poor Mr Slater died of his injuries.'

'Yes. Very sad. Let's hope they catch the thugs who did it.' *Preferably*, he prayed, *before they get around to me.*

'The police asked me to look at some photos of crimi-nals on their computer but frankly, they all looked the same — ugly and vicious. I wasn't much help, I'm afraid. I did remember that one of them had a foreign accent. They said that was useful.'

'What is it I can help you with, Monica?' Ludovic was alarmed at the foreign interest. He knew the crime gangs that

Rob dealt with had international contacts. In all probability, the operatives they'd employed to beat him to death were abroad by now and well out of reach of Detective Inspector Banerjee and his plods. But that didn't mean there weren't replacements waiting to take over. The organizations were infinite.

'It's been left to me to clear out Mr Slater's personal belongings. I'm all right with most of it, but I've found a gun. I didn't know he had one. What should I do with it? I didn't want to hand it over to the police, it seemed disloyal somehow. And they'd probably have asked lots of awkward questions. What do you think?'

'I think you were absolutely right not to say anything.' If the mob came for him, a gun could be just what he needed. It would, at least, make him feel safer. 'I'll dispose of it for you, shall I?'

'Yes, please. Thank you so much.' She rang off, thinking what a lovely man Mr de Coleville was. She envied his wife.

* * *

Ludovic turned the Glock over in his hand, getting a feel for the grip. He held it up and checked the sight alignment. Now that he had a weapon, he felt marginally better. He was pleased to see that it was an automatic. If the thugs turned up mob-handed, as they had with Rob, he was confident he could pick off a couple of them, hopefully scaring the rest before they had a chance to overpower him. He wondered why Rob hadn't used the gun to defend himself. Ludovic had learned to shoot at his public school and he was a tolerably good shot. He remembered Weedy Wilson had been terrified and would run away, blubbing, with his hands over his ears.

He intended to keep the gun loaded, ready to fire. Somewhere close at hand, where he could grab it in a hurry. Obviously, he couldn't afford for the police to find it, though he didn't think the police would get a second try at turning over the gallery without applying for a new warrant. To do that, they'd have to explain to the Justice of the Peace why they wanted a second one when the first one had produced nothing and they had no new evidence. Plus, they'd had the chance to arrest him and they hadn't, so he guessed they weren't as confident as Dawes and his fat sidekick appeared.

He glanced at the CCTV monitors. The gallery was busy. He had installed several security cameras on all three floors. He made a mental note to check the balustrade on the top floor. The last time he had been up there, it had looked as though the wood was deteriorating. He hoped it wasn't serious — any repairs to a listed building seemed to be exorbitant. He could see Sasha, on the ground floor, moving among the visitors, smiling and handing out brochures. He acknowledged that she was useful as a receptionist but it was time to move on. His solicitor had warned that she could take him to the cleaners if she had a halfway decent lawyer, but that was a battle for another day. Right now, his immediate problem was what to do with the large number of forgeries that were currently locked in his vault. He'd only ever been a go-between, obtaining the works from various contacts and passing them on to Rob. He had no idea where they went from there and he didn't want his first encounter with the organization to be his last. Rob had hinted that they weren't dealing with small time criminals. These were international firms — Serbs, Albanians, Ukrainians and the Mafia Românească, who had teamed up with UK mobsters. His exact words had been, *These guys make the Kray twins look like the Chuckle Brothers.*

Ludovic noticed a swarthy, bearded man, wearing jeans and a leather jacket, coming through the door. He stood out from the usual crowd, who were mainly middle-class and cultured. He watched Sasha approach him with a brochure, which he refused. He appeared to be telling her something and the smile left her face. He grinned, then turned and sauntered out.

Ludovic hurried down to speak to Sasha. 'What did that man want?'

She looked puzzled. 'I'm not sure. He said I was to tell you they would be back for their belongings, when the gallery wasn't so busy. He was very nasty and leered at me. Such an ugly man, tattoos all over his neck, scars on his face and a thick, foreign accent. I don't know what you've got yourself into Ludo, but I want no part of it.'

By now, Ludovic wanted no part of it, either, but how was he supposed to get out of it? Asking the police for help was out of the question. That fraud detective, Banerjee, would have him arrested and banged up in a heartbeat, never mind Dawes and his blasted Murder Investigation Team, trying to fit him up for the death of Parker. Briefly, he considered the possibility of dealing directly with the organization himself, now that they had effectively cut out the middle man, but it wasn't really an option. He didn't want to end up like Rob, nor did he want his gallery destroyed. He reckoned his only option was to hand over the forgeries in the vault when they turned up for them and keep the gun handy, in case things turned nasty.

He acknowledged that the pressure was getting to him. He seemed to spend most of the day with his eyes fixed on the CCTV monitor, waiting for gangsters to pile in. Rob must have told them about him and where he was when they were beating him up. Who could blame him? They'd found the gallery easily enough. Then there was Dawes telling him he was free to go *for now*, implying that they intended to arrest him when they had more evidence. Sometimes, he even thought he'd be safer in custody.

He had constant bellyache and had convinced himself that he was getting an ulcer from the stress. It was ridiculous and no way to carry on. He decided to close up the gallery for a few days and go away somewhere calming. It didn't matter where. Somewhere he could straighten himself out. The police hadn't said he couldn't leave Kings Richington without telling them and he had no intention of doing that. In the end, he decided on a spa hotel, where he could get massages and treatments from attractive women. They'd soon smooth out his kinks. He'd decide on the best way out of his situation when he was in a more rational frame of mind.

Bag packed, he made his way down the impressive staircase that was a striking feature of the de Coleville house on the Thames. He met Sasha on her way up. Anxious to get away, he simply said, 'I've closed up the gallery and I'm going out of town for a few days. You can do what you like.'

Sasha laughed scornfully. 'Those guys have really got you spooked, haven't they?'

'I don't know what you mean. I've just been working too hard and I need some time out.'

'When they catch up with you — and they will — I hope you get the kicking you deserve.' She carried on up the stairs, still laughing.

* * *

Back at the station, Jack was following up his intention to let de Coleville go, then put a tail on him to see what he did. He called across to DC Mitchell.

'Mitch, how d'you fancy a bit of 'obbo'? Follow de Coleville. Let me know where he goes and who he meets.'

'OK, guv. I'm on it.'

CHAPTER TWENTY-ONE

Modern-day Kings Richington was an affluent, self-satisfied town, nestled beside a quiet stretch of the Thames. It was sufficiently distant from the more urbanized developments of Hampton and Teddington to have become the favourite retreat of the rich and famous. Here were the luxury homes of judges, cabinet ministers, Harley Street surgeons and premiership football stars — none of whom read the *Richington Echo*. As Carlene had observed, orders from these customers were still frequent and lucrative. Bookings for dinner parties and soirées were coming in thick and fast, regardless of the bad press.

Corrie and Carlene were working in the main unit of Coriander's Cuisine. They were planning a dinner party menu for twenty and it had to be exceptionally elegant.

'What d'you reckon, Mrs D? Tournedos Rossini? Beef fillet, topped with foie gras served on a slice of toast, with a Madeira sauce drizzled over it? Maybe finished with a few truffle shavings. Customer says she really wants to serve Tournedos Rossini to impress her golfing buddies and their husbands, but she can't be arsed to fiddle with it.'

Corrie laughed. 'Is that what she actually said?'

'Well, no, but that's what it amounted to.'

'I thought maybe a strawberry mille-feuille for dessert,' suggested Corrie. 'Nice and summery to offset the richness of the Tournedos.' She was interrupted by vigorous knocking at the unit doors.

'Hello, can I come in?'

This was unusual. The main visitors to the unit were the staff and the drivers of the refrigerated vans who delivered raw ingredients.

Carlene and Corrie exchanged glances. Carlene put a finger to her lips and picked up a meat cleaver. Cautiously, she opened the door a crack, then sighed with relief.

'Hello, Mrs Garwood. Did you want to see Mrs Dawes? She's in the main kitchen.'

'Cynthia, how nice to see you. Have you come to book another garden party?' Corrie saw her face and grinned. 'I'm joking. Can we get you a coffee and a slice of Carlene's chocolate gâteau?'

'Well, I shouldn't, but yes, please. That would be lovely, Carlene. But I haven't come to scrounge food. It's about the garden party, actually. I know that appalling article in the *Echo* must have done you some harm. Who on earth did they get to write that rubbish? It was worse than the *Beano*. Anyway, I'm really sorry because I'm still convinced it wasn't your food that caused everyone to throw up.'

'So are we, Cynthia. We've racked our brains, haven't we, Carlene? Gone over every item, tested it to destruction, and we couldn't find anything. We even reconstructed the menu from the exact same ingredients and ate it ourselves, without any ill effects. Jack and Bugsy took some to the station and shared it around. Everyone was fine. We've drawn a blank, I'm afraid.'

'Well, I'm not a copper's wife for nothing and neither are you, Corrie. I think we should do some detective work.'

Corrie was touched. 'It's very kind of you to offer, but I think we've reached a dead end.'

'Not yet.' Cynthia was adamant. 'I still believe it was the jam I gave them that caused it. It can't be anything else.'

'Cynthia, we really don't think it's likely you'd get food poisoning from jam. Carlene did the module at college, didn't you?'

'That's right. "Fruit jam has a high sugar content that adds an extra measure of safety and a barrier to decomposition."'

'I'm sure you're right, Carlene, but suppose somebody put something in it? Something toxic?' Cynthia had the bit between her expensively whitened teeth.

'Like what?' asked Corrie.

'I don't know yet, but I think we should examine the possibility that it was done deliberately, don't you?'

'OK,' conceded Corrie. 'As a detective's wife, first I'd look for a motive — the reason why anyone would want to make a number of charity ladies sick. Then there's the means for committing the crime — in this case, jam. And lastly, opportunity — the occasion that presents itself, to allow the crime to take place, which was your garden party, Cynthia. For someone to become a suspect in a criminal investigation, we have to establish all three.'

'Maybe the motive was to ruin your reputation as a chef, Mrs D,' suggested Carlene. 'If that was the case, it's a rotten trick. Only you don't really have much competition round here. You're the best.'

Corrie frowned. 'Hang on a minute, you two. We're getting carried away with ourselves here. If someone did put something nasty in the jam to poison your ladies and discredit me, how could they be sure you'd serve it at your garden party? Even you didn't know you'd need it, until the raspberry ran out.'

Cynthia chewed her lip. 'Good point. Maybe it was really intended for me or George? If it had just been us that ate it, instead of being divided up between the little jam dishes, it might have been really dangerous. Maybe even fatal.'

Corrie thought Cynthia was galloping off into the realms of fantasy, like she often did. 'But who'd want to harm you or George? And even if they did, how would they get at your jam?'

'I expect lots of villains have a grudge against George, the number of criminals he's put away over the years. As for me, I'm standing for president of the Inner Wheel Club of Kings Richington. There's lots of cutthroat competition. In fact, some of them *would* cut your throat, if it meant getting elected. Putting poison in your jam would be tame. We have people in and out of the house all the time. Lots of folk could have access to my kitchen cupboard.'

Carlene had been quiet for a while. 'You said that you bought the jam from the Ladies' Guild stall on the market, Mrs Garwood?'

'That's right. I bought two jars, actually. George loves it — says it's the only jam with real strawberries in it.'

'What happened to the other jar?'

'We ate it. Had it on scones for tea in the garden, on Sunday.'

'And neither of you was ill?' asked Carlene.

Cynthia suddenly grasped the point. 'Oh, I see what you're getting at. If there *was* something in the jam, it was only in that one jar.'

'Not necessarily,' said Corrie, 'If it was added to the jam when it was being made, there could be several more poisoned jars out there, from that same batch.'

'But we haven't heard about anybody else eating strawberry jam and getting sick,' said Cynthia. 'No, I think the smart money is on someone putting it in just that one jar.'

Corrie nodded. 'Which again begs the question — why? What's the motive?'

'I suppose it could have been an accident,' said Carlene, without much conviction. 'We learned at college that some poisonous plants have healing powers in small amounts. Foxgloves, for example. What if the jam was made by some weirdo tree-hugger, who also makes herbal remedies? Maybe some poisonous gunk, that you're only meant to smear on your piles, got put in the jar with the jam?'

'If only we still had some,' lamented Corrie. 'We could get it tested by Forensics.'

'Right,' said Cynthia, firmly. 'Here's what we do, girls. Next Saturday morning, we go down to the market, interrogate the ladies on the Guild stall, and find out who made the jam. Once we know, we can decide what to do next. Are you in?'

'We're in,' they chorused.

* * *

On the following Saturday, two ladies from the other side of town were serving behind the Ladies' Guild counter. The market, as Carlene put it, was 'rammed,' so the three would-be detectives had to wait some time before the queue cleared.

Although Corrie used the market quite frequently, she didn't recognize the two ladies, and assumed they wouldn't recognize her, so Cynthia and Carlene put her in to bat first. As Cynthia pointed out, they didn't want to raise any suspicions. George always said people lie if they think they're under suspicion.

'Hello,' began Corrie. 'What lovely produce. Your members must be excellent cooks.'

'Not as good as you, Mrs Dawes.' Her Guild membership badge said she was called Joyce. 'My hubby and I have had takeaways from Corrie's Kitchen and they were delicious.'

That went well, thought Corrie. *So much for being anonymous.* 'Thank you, that's very kind. I'm so glad you enjoyed the food.'

'We didn't believe a word about you giving people food poisoning, did we, Joyce?' added her colleague.

'No, course we didn't. It said in the *Echo* that the party was at Cynthia Garwood's house. My cousin does the cleaning for her and she says her kitchen's a tip. Some days, you can't even see the worktop for dirty plates and stale food. It's a miracle she hasn't got rats. No wonder people were sick.'

Corrie decided to change the subject pretty rapidly. 'I've actually come to buy some of your strawberry jam. I've heard it's delicious.'

'Certainly, Mrs Dawes. How many jars do you need? Mrs Wilson, our president, makes the strawberry jam but she hasn't brought any in lately, on account of her mother-in-law dying. Heart attack, I believe. She said it was peaceful, though. We've got a couple of jars and there's plenty of raspberry.'

'Thank you, I'll take two jars of each.'

* * *

Corrie reported back to her co-conspirators, who were enjoying coffee and Danish pastries at a stall further down the market.

'Right, ladies, we have the name of the person who made the jam. She's Mrs Wilson and she's the current president of the Guild.'

Carlene was already on her phone, googling the Kings Richington Ladies' Guild executive board. 'Her name's Fenella Wilson and she has her own website. As well as being president, she's a self-employed illustrator of children's books. She's married to David Wilson, a human resources manager, and they don't have any kids.'

'I bought two jars of her strawberry jam. She hasn't delivered her usual batch this weekend as she's suffered a bereavement,' said Corrie. 'Her mother-in-law died of a heart attack.'

'That's a surprising amount of information for a five-minute visit,' remarked Cynthia. 'I'm impressed.'

Corrie thought she'd be less impressed if she told her the bit about her kitchen being a tip. 'Now we know who made the jam, what next? I think it very unlikely that this Mrs Wilson tampered with it — a president and paradigm of propriety. Why would she? If the poison was in the jam — and we don't know for sure that it was — it must have been put in afterwards.'

'I doubt if anyone could have fiddled with it once it was set out on the stall. The ladies work in twos, and someone would have noticed. I wonder if it goes anywhere else. I think we should pay Mrs Wilson a visit, ask a few discreet questions,' suggested Cynthia.

'On what pretext?' asked Corrie.

'We'll say we're interested in joining the Guild and that someone mentioned she'd be the person to talk to.'

'It's got her email address on here but not where she lives,' reported Carlene. 'We can easily find out, though.'

'We'll give her time to get over her mother-in-law's death, then we'll pop round.'

CHAPTER TWENTY-TWO

Fenella was rehearsing the plan to put poison in David's Ovaltine. It had to go perfectly and it had to be done soon, before the bastard legged it abroad. She didn't know if he had plans to change his will. Having said that, who was he going to leave all that money to? Not Sasha, surely? That would be the ultimate insult. She had to put a stop to that. Even if he'd gone so far as to push through probate and the money was already in his account, if he died now, it would come to his wife, as next of kin.

It was while she was thrashing all this out in her mind that the doorbell rang. David was out, as he always seemed to be these days, either with his tart or organizing Ida's flight to Rome, and in any case, he had a key, so he wouldn't have rung the bell.

When she opened the door to find Cynthia, Corrie and Carlene standing there, she stepped back and tottered slightly. She recognized Cynthia Garwood from the frequent photos of her alongside her husband in the *Echo*, and her equally frequent visits to the stall. Corrie Dawes, she knew by reputation and she'd seen her at the market, too. The other girl was the one who worked in Corrie's Kitchen. What was the deputation all about? It could only be that they had somehow found out that it was her jam that had poisoned the ladies at Cynthia Garwood's party and harmed Corrie Dawes's reputation as a chef. The game was up. They couldn't have found out about poor old Jericho and Ida's untimely demise, could they? As long as it was only the food-poisoning episode, she thought she could, if she had to, pass it off as a terrible accident. *Hold your nerve, Fenella*, she told herself. *That's what Jude would say.*

'Mrs Wilson,' began Cynthia. 'I do hope you don't mind us calling, uninvited, like this. One of your members on the Ladies' Guild stall mentioned that you were the president this year.'

'Er — yes, that's right,' began Fenella cautiously.

'We wondered,' said Corrie, 'whether you could give us some information about how we might go about joining — that's if you'll have us, of course.' Corrie indicated the three of them, thinking that it was starting to feel like the opening scene of Macbeth, with the three witches. *Fair is foul, and foul is fair. Too right*, she thought.

Fenella didn't know what to think. It could be that they were genuinely interested in joining the Guild, or was it a fact-finding mission to trap her? She needed time to think.

'How lovely! I'm sure the Guild would be very pleased to have you. Please come in and I'll make some tea. Then we can discuss your membership.'

After she had disappeared into the kitchen, they spoke in hushed tones.

'What d'you reckon, girls?' whispered Cynthia.

'Seems like a perfectly nice woman to me,' Corrie whispered back.

'Not the sort to put poison in a chap's jam, then,' agreed Cynthia.

'Could still have been an accident,' muttered Carlene. 'I'll just nip through and take a look at her kitchen. I want to see if she makes anything else — like haemorrhoid cream from hemlock.'

Cynthia and Corrie could hear Carlene asking, 'Can I help with that, Mrs Wilson?'

Fenella returned with the tea tray and cake followed by Carlene with the teapot. Behind Fenella's back, she shook her head at the others.

After a pleasant half-hour discussing the various functions of the Guild and how the three ladies might contribute, Fenella showed them out and breathed a sigh of relief. She was confident, now, that they had come for the reason they had given. And even if they hadn't, she remembered what Jude had said about the jam — *There's no way it can be traced back to you.*

* * *

Back at Coriander's Cuisine, the three conspirators were conferring. Corrie was remembering what Joyce's mate's cousin had said about the state of Cynthia's kitchen. 'How well do you get on with your cleaner, Cynthia?' she asked.

Cynthia shrugged. 'She's OK, I suppose. Hadn't really thought about it. I'm hardly ever there when she cleans, I just leave her the money. Why?'

'Oh, nothing really. Just something one of the Guild Ladies said.' Corrie wasn't about to tell her or she suspected the poor girl would find herself out of a job.

'You don't think my cleaner put poison in my jam?' Cynthia asked, incredulous.

'Anything's possible. She's not standing for election as president of the Inner Wheel Club, is she?'

'Oh — I see where you're going. No, I doubt it. She's more your bingo and burger girl.'

'Might George have nicked her dad or her granddad or any other members of her family, at some time?'

'It's possible, I suppose. George was never fussy who he nicked, as long as it looked good on the end-of-month returns.'

Carlene was dipping a spoon in a jar of strawberry jam and tasting it. 'Well, I've had three spoonfuls of this and I feel fine.'

'Where did you get that?' chorused Cynthia and Corrie.

'I pinched it from Mrs Wilson's store cupboard while she was getting the tea.' She saw their horrified faces. 'Well, it's no use being a sleuth if you don't inspect the evidence.'

* * *

As soon as Cynthia, Corrie and Carlene had gone, Fenella went to see Judith. She needed to tell her that she thought they were on to her.

'Did they mention jam?' Judith asked.

'No, not once.'

'So why did you think they'd come to accuse you?' Judith asked.

'I don't know. Guilt, I suppose. You know what it's like when you've done something wrong? You lie awake at night imagining people will find out and you'll get caught. Then, as soon as something out of the ordinary happens, you automatically assume the worst.'

'Stop worrying.' Judith opened a bottle. 'They're respectable ladies, the sort who might easily want to join the Guild. In fact, if Corrie Dawes wants to contribute any produce to the stall, we're quids in. People will flock to buy it.'

'Even though they think her food poisoned people?' suggested Fenella.

'But we know that wasn't true, don't we? And folk soon forget — especially if they get to buy haute cuisine at a knock-down price. Have a glass of this Merlot and relax.'

Fenella swallowed several large mouthfuls and felt better. 'Mostly, I'm wondering if I should go ahead with David's . . . you know, *project*. It's a bit awkward, two of my relatives dying so close together. Do you think when the police find him, they'll be suspicious? Corrie Dawes's husband is an inspector in the murder squad.'

'If we do it properly, the only person they'll suspect will be David — of suicide. You'll emphasize how depressed he was following his mother's death. Explain how close they were and how worried you'd been about his mental health.'

'What about Sasha de Coleville? Won't she tell the coroner that they'd been having a jolly little affair? Lots of rumpy-pumpy, and him with his new sexy, leopard print thongs.'

'Then you counter that by telling them it was just another symptom of his deep depression. A desperate need to try and replace his mother with someone who would flatter and indulge him, like Ida did. You were his wife for fifteen years, they'll believe you, not his bit on the side.'

'I wish I could think on my feet like you, Jude.'

'Listen, I'll be right there with you, the whole time. Perfectly natural for a grieving widow to be comforted by her best friend. And we really need to get on with this, before he has a chance to leave the country and take the money with him.'

'Yes, I know. He said that as soon as he'd got everything sorted, he'd be away. I've seen his ticket — he's going on Monday. I'll do it at the weekend.'

CHAPTER TWENTY-THREE

The Murder Investigation Team was working through all the intelligence they had on de Coleville's connection with Slater. Detective Inspector Banerjee's team had already examined both men's finances and they had found nothing to indicate any activity beyond the normal running of the two art galleries.

'The money must be going somewhere,' decided DC Williams. 'Clive has hacked into everything in the de Coleville business accounts and also those of his wife, Sasha, in case he's hiding the cash in her name.'

'Anything about the organized-crime gangs that Slater might have had — although I doubt if he was careless enough to keep names and locations — was destroyed during the raid. They covered their tracks very well,' observed Jack.

'These men are professionals. They don't make mistakes,' said DC Fox.

'All crooks make mistakes eventually, Gemma,' said Bugsy. 'It's a weakness of the criminal mind. Sooner or later, they start to believe they're Teflon-coated and that's when they let their guard down.'

'Sergeant Malone's right,' confirmed Dawes. 'You'd be surprised how many of the Kray Twins' firm were caught, because they got careless and bragged to the wrong people about how clever they were.'

'Excuse me, sir.' DC Williams called across to Jack. 'DC Mitchell has just reported in. He says chummy is on the move. He locked up the gallery and got in his car, carrying what looked like an overnight bag. Mitch has followed him to' — he consulted his notes — 'the Seventh Heaven Spa Hotel. What do you want him to do, sir?'

'Tell Mitch to show his badge, discreetly, at reception and find out how long de Coleville has booked in for.'

'Sir.' Aled passed the message on. Fifteen minutes later, he reported back. 'De Coleville has booked in for a week. The receptionist said he's having the full range of treatments, working his way right through the menu. Lymphatic stimulation, "Men's grooming experience" — back, sack and crack — deep tissue de-stress massage, Reiki, acupuncture. Must be costing a bomb, Mitch says. He's seen the price list.'

'OK, tell Mitch he can come back in. Unless de Coleville plans to meet his criminal contacts in the sauna, I guess we can leave him for now.'

'If we can't nail him for anything else, I still want to get him for "manslaughter as the result of an unlawful act",' said Bugsy.

'I think we'll find he's up to his neck in much more than that,' said Jack. 'While he's having his nails manicured, I think Detective Inspector Banerjee and our team should have another look round the gallery. What I don't want is for the mob to nail him before we can.'

'Do you reckon they already know about the Coleville Gallery, sir?' asked Gemma.

'Almost certainly. If Slater didn't tell them when they were beating him up, they'd have found something in the office. Monica may have said something, although I doubt it because she obviously fancies de Coleville.'

'Might be tricky getting another warrant,' said Bugsy. 'Ash has already given the place a spin without finding anything.'

Thanks to his rugby past, Jack's grin was lopsided on a good day, but even more so when he was contemplating something unorthodox. 'I don't think we need bother with procedure on this occasion, Sergeant. We know de Coleville is out of the way for a while and I doubt whether Mrs de Coleville will spend any time in the gallery, if she doesn't have to. We'll go late at night, when it's dark, and have a discreet look around.'

'Won't there be alarms and CCTV, sir?' asked Gemma.

'Absolutely. I think Clive has that covered.'

Clive looked up from his screen. 'Yep. I've hacked into the security system, sir. Not as sophisticated as you'd expect. I can switch it off and back on again from my laptop, whenever you give the word. The vault was trickier, it's encased in concrete and steel, but I've cracked it. As for lights inside the gallery, some are left on all night to make surveillance easier, when Sergeant Parsloe's officers patrol the area.'

'Well done. If anybody sees us moving about, they'll just think de Coleville's doing a stocktake or something. Even if someone rings in to report it, we'll get the call as the closest car to the scene. We'll say we went in to investigate in response to a call from a concerned member of the public. Right, is everyone on for tonight? Overtime, naturally. Get Mitch on board. The more of us there are, the quicker we can do the job. I'll contact Ash and his lads.'

* * *

It was late and Corrie was at a loose end. Jack was working overtime and didn't know when he'd be back. He'd told her not to wait up and to have supper without him. She had no idea what job the team was on, but she got the impression it was something covert, so hadn't asked. Just as she was trying to make up her mind between some leftover *poulet parmentier* and beans on toast, her phone rang. Cynthia Garwood's number came up.

'Hello, Cynthia. How are you?'

'Bored and hungry. Georgie is out at a Masonic dinner and won't be home until late. Is Chez Carlene open tonight?'

'Yes, the bistro's open until midnight on Fridays.'

'Do you fancy having supper out? I know you're capable of rustling up an eight-course banquet in ten minutes without breaking a sweat, but I thought it might be nice if we didn't have to cook for a change.'

Corrie smiled to herself. Cynthia never cooked — she didn't know how. 'As it happens, Jack's working overtime tonight. I've no idea when he'll be home, so yes, that would be good. Shall I pick you up, so you can have some wine?'

Chez Carlene occupied the entire corner of Kings Richington high street, with windows all around. In the summer, there were tables outside under a striped, yellow awning. Inside, it was decorated in Parisian style — strongly influenced by Antoine — so that customers felt they might almost be dining on the Left Bank. By day, it was a brasserie, cool and dark with mottled, sea-green tabletops and French accordion music, playing softly in the background. At night, it turned into a bustling bistro, an urban creation, loud and relaxed, where customers might saunter in wearing T-shirts and shorts. The menu was simple but superbly executed, with classic fare such as coq au vin with potato gratin, or lighter dishes, like an omelette or croque monsieur. It had taken off immediately, and had captured the imagination of Kings Richington folk — young and old. Corrie was immensely proud of the way Carlene and Antoine ran it.

It was half past ten by the time Cynthia and Corrie arrived, and the bistro was still heaving with noisy, cheerful customers. They found a table in the window and Carlene came over as soon as she saw them.

'Hello, Mrs Garwood, Mrs D. We don't often see you in here at this time of night. What can I get you?'

'Anything,' groaned Cynthia. 'I'm so hungry, I could eat this table mat.'

'How about sharing a bowl of moules marinières and some crusty bread, while you're deciding?'

'Wonderful!' they chorused.

Cynthia had a carafe of house white with the mussels and by the time the boeuf bourguignon arrived, she was feeling much happier. 'I'll have a carafe of red with this, please, Carlene.'

Carlene glanced at Corrie but she just shrugged and raised her eyebrows. By the time the desserts came, Cynthia was doing an Edith Piaf impression to the Parisian accordion music.

'Non, je ne regrette rien . . .'

I think you might in the morning, thought Corrie.

* * *

At ten minutes to midnight, a black Mercedes people carrier edged its way down Kings Richington high street and cruised around the corner. It passed the bistro window, unnoticed by Cynthia and Corrie, who were sitting finishing their coffee. The vehicle pulled up in the unlit alleyway, behind the Coleville Gallery, and six men climbed out. They were armed with various heavy implements, capable of breaking down doors and windows. The men had made no attempt to conceal their identity and wore ordinary clothes — jeans, jackets, hoodies and heavy boots.

The gang leader motioned to them to break down the double doors. From there, they smashed their way in through the back of the gallery, disabling the alarms by shattering them with baseball bats.

Once inside, they made as if to destroy the exhibits, as the thugs had in the Slater Gallery, but the boss stopped them. 'Don't waste time on this rubbish. It has little value to the organization. We're here to find the forgeries Slater told us about.'

They searched all three floors, shouting to each other that they'd found nothing. Just as they were thinking it was a wasted effort, the ugly one with scars and tattoos shouted up from the cellar.

'It's down here. Come down here.'

He had found the vault.

Ludovic had spared no expense installing it, conscious of the type of merchandise he intended it to contain. It was an integral part of the building, sited on a reinforced concrete floor with individual, armoured steel walls and ceiling welded into place. The door closed electronically with alarms and an anti-theft device.

'What we are looking for is in here. We've got to get inside.'

They bashed at it for a while, using every tool they had, but making no impression whatsoever. Even gangsters know when they're beaten. No amount of brute force would open the door.

Finally, one of the henchmen spoke. 'We're wasting time, *şef*. We need welding equipment at least, to get in here.'

'The quickest way would be to find de Coleville. I'll make him open it,' boasted a muscle-bound thug, cracking his knuckles.

They had already been to de Coleville's house on the river. It had been in darkness, apart from the outside security lights. They had shouted, pounded on the door and broken a few windows but it was clear nobody was home nor were there any vehicles outside. The house was in a rural position on the Thames where walking anywhere wasn't really an option. They were standing, looking helplessly at the vault, when they heard voices upstairs in the gallery.

CHAPTER TWENTY-FOUR

Corrie had left her car in a car park, some distance down the street from Chez Carlene. She and Cynthia waited for Carlene to close up and offered her a lift home. The three ladies linked arms, with Cynthia in the middle, as she felt a little unsteady, after the night air hit her.

'Smashing grub, Carlene,' she said, rather louder than necessary. 'Best I've ever had.' She remembered Corrie. 'Apart from yours, of course. Brilliant chefs, both of you. Don't know how you do it.'

'We could teach you,' offered Corrie, more in hope than expectation.

'That's an idea, Mrs D,' said Carlene. 'Maybe we could start posh, cookery courses for ladies who entertain — Coriander's School of Food and Wine.'

You have to hand it to her, thought Corrie. She was the consummate entrepreneur, always thinking up new ways to expand the business.

'We could start a course for blokes — Make Your Own Takeaway. Mind you, if they got too good at it, they wouldn't need to come to us, so maybe . . .' she stopped in her tracks as they entered the unlit alleyway, which was the short cut to the car park. 'Mrs D, look at that. Someone's broken into the Coleville Gallery. The back doors are all smashed up.'

Corrie looked. 'Blimey, you're right. What a mess. Well, it isn't safe to leave it like that, even if it is full of junk art. I'll ring Jack.' She pulled out her phone and punched in his mobile number but it went straight to voicemail. She called his station phone.

Cynthia giggled. 'Georgie'll have a fit when he finds out somebody's done a burgle-ry — I mean, a burglary on his patch. He'll be chewing indigestion tablets for a week, bless him.'

'Hello.' Corrie finally got through to the station. It seemed that no one was answering the MIT phones. It sounded like she'd got one of the cleaners. 'Oh, I see. Well, thanks anyway.' She turned to Carlene and Cynthia. 'Apparently, everyone except the switchboard operator is out on a job and he doesn't know where. He said he'd try to contact the team by radio and pass on my message about the break-in.'

'What we gonna do?' slurred Cynthia.

'I think we should go inside, try to make it secure and I'll keep trying Jack's mobile, until someone comes,' suggested Corrie.

'Top-hole, girls,' giggled Cynthia. 'The three C's save the day!'

Corrie sighed. 'Do get a grip, Cynthia, you sound like an Enid Blyton novel. Come on, we'll stand guard until the cops get here.'

'OK, Mrs D. Sounds like a plan.' Carlene led the way and they climbed over the splintered doors, passing through the lobby and into the main floor of the gallery.

'It doesn't look like they've nicked anything,' said Carlene, looking around.

'No, it doesn't, does it?' agreed Corrie. 'Maybe whoever broke in came for something specific but didn't find it, so they left empty-handed.'

'I need a wee,' said Cynthia, legs crossed. 'There must be loos in here.'

'You don't want to use the public ones, Mrs Garwood. You should see the state of the bogs in Chez Carlene at this time of night, before the cleaners have had a go.' She pointed to a door with 'Staff Only' on it. 'There's bound to be a decent one in there.'

They went into the staffroom, and while Corrie tried Jack's phone again, Cynthia nipped into the loo.

'Still no joy, Mrs D?'

'Nope. Still voicemail. What can they be doing? It's well past midnight.'

* * *

The convoy of unmarked police cars was making its way, unobtrusively, into Kings Richington, via the back roads. DC Williams got a call on his radio.

'Right, thanks. I'll tell the boss.' He turned to speak to Jack who was in the back with Bugsy. 'Sir, that was Clive. He says something funny's going on in the gallery. He was logged in, waiting for your command to turn off the security, when it suddenly went off on its own — all except the vault. That's still locked.'

'Maybe de Coleville came back,' said Bugsy.

'Why would he do that?' asked Mitch, who was driving. 'He's paid for a week's worth of treatments.'

'Could be Mrs de Coleville,' said Jack.

'I doubt it' said Bugsy. 'From what Ash told us, she didn't much want to be there at all, never mind at night.'

'We'll be there soon, said Mitch. 'Do you want me to put my foot down, guv? Blues and twos?'

'No, don't do that,' said Jack. 'It's probably just a power cut or something. We don't want to put the wind up the whole of Kings Richington at this time of night. Just cruise gently into town and we'll sort it out when we get there.'

* * *

The gang leader put a finger to his lips to tell the others to keep quiet. He could hear muffled voices coming from above. He motioned to the others to follow and crept up the stairs — then he kicked open the staffroom door.

Confronted by six menacing thugs carrying clubs and coshes, Corrie and Carlene were understandably alarmed, but tried not to show it.

'Who are you and what are you doing here?' demanded Corrie, with a bravado she wasn't feeling.

The gang leader grinned. 'We might ask you the same,' he countered. When he'd heard the murmurs from above, he thought it might have been the police and had anticipated a pitched battle to get away. Now he could see it was only a couple of women, he relaxed.

'Well, we didn't break in, like you,' snapped Carlene. 'We've phoned the police and they're on the way. You'd better run for it while you can.'

He turned to his gang, who had surrounded Corrie and Carlene in the staffroom. 'What are we going to do with these two chickens, guys?'

A particularly ugly and sweaty brute bore down on Carlene. 'I know what I'd like to do with this one.' He leered at her.

'You leave her alone,' demanded Corrie, 'or you'll be sorry. My husband is a police officer and if you touch her, he'll hunt you down.'

This was apparently amusing, as all six men burst into howls of unpleasant laughter.

Meanwhile, in the staff toilet and oblivious to what was going on, Cynthia was looking for a towel to dry her hands. She pulled open the cupboard door under the washbasin and saw what she believed to be a folded guest towel. She tugged at it. A gun fell out. Despite being married to a police chief, Cynthia had little knowledge of weapons. She picked it up, gingerly. *I bet de Coleville doesn't have a licence for this*, she thought. *And even if he does, he has no business keeping it in a bathroom cupboard. George says that guns should be locked away in a metal cabinet.* She was just trying to decide what was best to do with it when she heard the roars of male laughter outside the door. *Oh good,* she thought. *Corrie must have got through to Jack and the police are here. Jack will know what to do with the gun.*

She threw open the door. 'Look what I've found . . .' She saw a big, sweaty ruffian wrestling with Carlene and Corrie struggling to get free from the gang leader. Horrified, she levelled the gun at the men, holding it in both hands. They backed off, nervously. Men with guns were dangerous. Women with guns were lethal.

'Let them go or I'll shoot,' she screamed. Her finger had barely touched the hair trigger, when the faulty gun immediately began to fire in rapid bursts. Cynthia screamed, over and over, and spun around in terrified circles, spraying the room with bullets. The men, not surprisingly, lost interest in Corrie and Carlene. Some ducked under the desk while others dived into the loo. Two of the biggest got wedged in the doorway in their bid to be anywhere out of range of the random hail of bullets. Cynthia didn't stop firing until she'd emptied the magazine — all thirteen rounds.

* * *

Outside, the convoy of police cars was pulling up outside the gallery, as quietly as they could. Aled's radio bleeped. He spoke briefly, then reported to Jack.

'Sir, that was the station. They've had a call from Mrs Dawes. She said the Coleville Gallery has been broken into. She's in there now, with Mrs Garwood and Carlene.'

'Bloody hell!' groaned Jack. 'What the devil are Corrie and her mates doing here?'

'Best we get in there and find out, guv,' said Bugsy.

Mitch agreed. 'Gives us a legitimate reason for being here.'

As the officers piled out, they heard gunfire coming from inside. Jack and Bugsy exchanged a split-second glance then broke into a sprint with the other coppers hard on their heels. They raced inside, dreading what they'd find. It was pandemonium. Cynthia was still screaming and Carlene was punching the ruffian, who would certainly have assaulted her, if Cynthia hadn't shot off his earlobe. He was bleeding profusely and shouting foreign obscenities. The gang leader was bent double with tears in his eyes, having received Corrie's well-aimed knee in his crotch. The rest of the gang made a dash for freedom, straight into the arms of the officers rushing in.

Unwilling to give up without a fight, the six men clashed violently with the charging police. Despite their arsenal of clubs and coshes, they were no match for trained officers with batons. For several minutes, the gallery resounded with yells of pain and cursing and the crunch of wooden sticks meeting flesh and bone.

Finally, it was all over and the gang was led away, bloodied and bruised, in handcuffs.

Corrie hurled herself into Jack's arms. 'Thank God you're here. I really thought we were going to die.'

He held her tightly. 'Did the bastards threaten to kill you, sweetheart?'

'No — I thought Cynthia was going to shoot us all.'

Bugsy looked around at the damage. One bullet had gone straight through the water cooler, which was leaking all over the floor. Another had shattered the CCTV monitor and two more were embedded in the door frame. One had even travelled through the open door into the portrait gallery and shot out Lord Nelson's good eye.

Bugsy whistled. 'Blimey, guv, talk about *Gunfight at the OK Corral*.' He went across to where Carlene was attempting to comfort Cynthia. She was still shaking but her screams had died down to a whimper. 'Mrs Garwood, didn't it occur to you to just drop the gun?'

'No . . . no . . . I couldn't let go,' Cynthia sobbed. 'It just kept spinning me around and it wouldn't stop firing.'

He looked down. 'Carlene, love, you've got blood on your leg.'

She grinned. 'That'll be from the bloke I was wrestling with. Mrs Garwood shot his ear off. He didn't half bleed.'

Bugsy bent down. 'No, love, you've been wounded.'

'Oh, Carlene, I shot you. I'm so sorry,' Cynthia wailed.

'It'll just be a nick,' said Carlene. 'Nothing to worry about.'

'I think it is, love,' said Bugsy. 'The bullet has gone right through your calf muscle.'

She looked down at the blood, rapidly soaking through her jeans and dripping onto the floor. 'Oh bugger, I think I'm going to . . .'

Bugsy caught her before she hit the floor.

CHAPTER TWENTY-FIVE

News of the shoot-out travelled fast. Half an hour after the ambulance had taken Carlene to hospital, with Corrie in attendance, Jack got a call.

'Dawes, what the blazes is going on?' Chief Superintendent Garwood had returned home from his Masonic dinner, replete and mellow from several glasses of excellent port, only to find a message on his answerphone, urging him to contact the station. 'Uniform have just informed me that you are attending a firearms incident at the Coleville Gallery.'

'That's right, sir.'

'Have you called out the Specialist Firearms Unit?'

'No, sir, I didn't think it necessary.'

'Why ever not, man? These officers are specially trained to fire upon a suspect, if they pose an immediate threat to life. Do you have an armed criminal brandishing a firearm at a member of the public?'

'Not any longer, sir. She has handed it over.'

'She? *She*? Do you mean the criminal is a woman?'

'That's right, sir.' Jack wondered how he was going to break it to him.

'Is she a known terrorist? Do we have an identity?'

'No, she isn't a terrorist, sir — and yes, we do have an identity.'

'Well?'

Jack took a deep breath. 'It's Mrs Garwood.'

'Don't be ridiculous, Dawes. My wife's upstairs in bed. I was just about to go up myself.'

'No, she isn't, sir. She's here with a blanket round her, waiting for you to come and take her home. She'll explain everything. I doubt there will be any charges. Nobody died, but there were a couple of injuries. Shall I tell her you're on your way?'

Garwood put down the phone, took out a packet of indigestion tablets and ate six, straight off. Whatever would the *Echo* make of this?

* * *

Detective Inspector Banerjee and his men had made straight for the cellar. They were going through the contents of the vault, which Clive and his laptop had obligingly opened for them. Jack went down to see what they'd found.

Ash looked pleased. 'The last time we were here with a warrant, de Coleville had emptied it before we could search. We're assuming the last lot went up in smoke together with Parker, so this must be another consignment. Look at all this, Jack.' There were paintings, sculptures, Chinese porcelain — all forgeries. 'There's serious money here. Art and Antiques are confiscating the lot, my lads are loading it into the vans right now. A couple of my team have gone to the Seventh Heaven Spa Hotel to pick him up.'

'That'll give him a shock — coppers knocking on the door of his hotel room at two in the morning,' observed Jack.

'I'm not giving him the chance to leg it this time. If I leave it until morning, his wife might tip him off,' said Ash.

'That's if she knows where he is,' said Bugsy. 'I got the impression she wouldn't warn him, even when she hears about the raid on the gallery.'

Ash nodded. 'You're right. There's no love lost there. I'll let him stew in a cell until morning, then I shall be wanting answers to some serious questions about his suppliers.'

'I wonder how he was intending to shift it, now that Slater's dead?' said Bugsy.

'Whatever he was planning, I doubt if he was expecting some of the mob to come and collect it,' observed Aled. 'Lucky for him he was out of the way.'

'I reckon he'd have just handed it over. You saw those six goons that were sent to get it.' Bugsy pulled a fluff-covered sausage roll from his pocket — one of several provided by Iris when he said he'd be late home. 'You don't argue with them if you value your gonads.'

'My wife did,' said Jack, morosely. 'And Mr Garwood's wife. And Carlene. She'd take on an army, if they threatened Corrie.'

'Thank God they're all safe,' said Bugsy, 'although Carlene was complaining that her designer jeans were ruined. I don't understand it, myself. What's a couple of bullet holes when they were already ripped?'

* * *

Ludovic de Coleville had spent a relaxing day at the spa, having his chakras realigned. According to Cloud, the delightful young lady who had been looking after him, he had moved away from a harmonized state of being and was at risk of both physical and mental illness as a result. She asked if he had recently experienced anger issues, anxiety or low libido. *Sweetheart, you have no idea*, he thought. By midnight, she had unblocked all his chakras and he was sleeping like a baby.

At half past two, he was awoken by gentle tapping on his door. At first, he thought he had dreamt it but it got louder. Then the manager's voice called to him in a hoarse whisper.

'Mr de Coleville. I'm sorry to disturb you but there are two police officers here to see you. I'm afraid they are insisting they can't wait until morning.'

'Just open the door for us, please, sir,' said the sergeant.

The manager did as he was told, not wanting any trouble with the police or an unpleasant altercation that might disturb the other guests.

Dazed, Ludovic sat up and reached for his dressing gown just as the police officers came in. The constable stood by the door while the sergeant made the arrest. 'Get dressed please, Mr de Coleville. My orders are to take you back to the station.'

Ludovic dressed slowly, his mind in turmoil, wondering what the hell had gone wrong. The copper had said he was being arrested on suspicion of dealing in forged art and antiques and being in possession of a gun. They had no evidence — or they hadn't when he left. Slater was dead so it couldn't have been him. Sasha's knowledge was limited, it wasn't enough to give the police the confidence to arrest him. He got his belongings together and followed the officers down to the car.

'What exactly is it you think I've done, officer?' It was the tone Ludovic used when he wanted to come across as genuine but misunderstood.

'I'm afraid I'm not at liberty to discuss it, sir. The Detective Inspector will interview you later. Mind your head.' He shoved him into the back of the police car.

* * *

Ludovic was duly processed and put in a cell. A few hours later, they brought him breakfast, which was greasy and disgusting. He contented himself with a plastic cup of coffee, which was equally disgusting but better than nothing. He used his one phone call to contact his solicitor. Caroline Jackson arrived half an hour later.

'What have you been up to, Ludo? You've been arrested because forged paintings and other fake artefacts have been found in a vault in the cellar of your gallery. There's also an allegation that a handgun was found in a cupboard in the staff washroom. Is this true? You must be honest with me, if I'm going to represent you.'

Ludovic thought fast. 'It's true that I had some stock in the cellar, Caro, but as far as I knew, they were absolutely genuine. I mean, why would I keep them under lock and key, if they were worthless fakes? As for the gun, I was asked by Rob Slater's receptionist to dispose of it for her, after the Slater Gallery closed.' Ludovic had been tempted to say that he knew nothing about any gun and the woman who claimed she found it, then apparently fired it, like a demented Annie Oakley, must have brought it with her. However, when he'd discovered the woman was the wife of a senior police officer, he didn't think he'd get away with it. Added to which, if they questioned Monica, she would undoubtedly tell the truth.

She sniffed. 'I don't think that's going to cut it. I've spoken to Detective Inspector Banerjee and being disingenuous won't work. You and I both know that art fraud isn't about flamboyant forgers in smocks and berets, but organized international gangs, and six members of one such gang were arrested inside your gallery.'

'I've no idea who those men were. Can't I claim that I'm the innocent party in all this? Just a poor gallery owner, trying to make a decent living?'

'You're wasting your time if you think you can bamboozle the police with your air of gentlemanly bravado. You won't persuade them that making money from the forgeries of great masters is forgivable, or a lesser crime than "ordinary" fraud.' She opened a file and began writing. 'I don't suppose you have paperwork to support your claim that you purchased this merchandise in good faith? No, I didn't think so. What about a list of the suppliers who provided the stuff? That's another no, then.'

Ludovic put his head in his hands. 'I was just the middle man, Caro. Rob Slater had the contacts in the underworld. I delivered the stuff to him but I've no idea where it went after that.'

She stood up. 'OK, Ludo, I think we're into damage limitation here, but unless we box clever, we're on a hiding to nothing. Only answer their questions if I tell you.'

* * *

The six men arrested at the gallery were in custody and were saying nothing. It was clear that they were far more afraid of what would happen to them and their families if they talked, than they were of British police officers. Since none of them was in the UK legally, they believed the worst that could happen would be that they'd be deported. Even though a couple of them had very little English, they had been taught to chant, 'No comment' effectively. Detective Inspector Banerjee was pleased with the haul but knew it was the tip of a monumental iceberg.

'We showed Monica from the Slater Gallery photos of the blokes, in the hope that she might be able to pick out the three who effectively killed Slater. She didn't recognize any of them, so they were from a different firm.'

'The mob will have moved them on — probably abroad by now,' said Jack.

Ash nodded. 'We ran the prints and DNA of our six through the database but none of them is known to us. These organized-crime gangs have access to a huge workforce. If some of them are arrested, so what? They just recruit more. They have such a loose hierarchy that the chances of ever identifying the real bosses are remote — but we have to keep trying.'

'Any joy with the black Mercedes people carrier?' asked Bugsy.

'Stolen last night from outside a funeral parlour. Forensics are going over it but they don't reckon on finding anything useful.'

'Shall we have a crack at chummy now?' asked Jack.

'Yep. I suggest a two-pronged interrogation. I'll start by asking him about the forgeries in the gallery, then you and

Bugsy can come out of left field and tackle him about the arson.'

When they went into the interview room, Jack was daunted to see Caroline Jackson. She was well-known to the police for taking an active part in the interrogation, unlike those they often saw who sat quietly beside their client scribbling in a file, who don't even look up, let alone give advice. Caroline Jackson was not one of these.

Banerjee began. 'You are here, Mr de Coleville, because you have been arrested on suspicion of involvement in art fraud and possession of an unlicensed firearm. Can you tell us what you know about the items we found in your vault?'

'You don't have to answer that,' said Caroline immediately. 'This isn't a fishing expedition, gentlemen. Please ask direct questions.'

Ash pushed some photographs across the table. 'These are some of the items found in your cellar, Mr de Coleville. Do you recognize them?'

'Er — no. I've been away for few days. They certainly weren't there when I left. Someone else must have put them in there while I was gone.' He looked at Caroline, who nodded.

'But your vault is protected by several sophisticated security devices. How would anyone, apart from you, be able to get into it?' challenged Ash.

'Well, *you* did, officer,' Caroline countered. 'My client didn't give you the electronic access details. If you were able to hack in, so might someone else have.'

'Why would anyone want to plant forgeries in your gallery?' asked Ash, beginning to get rattled.

Caroline jumped in before Ludovic could say anything. 'I suggest that's for the police to establish. You surely don't expect my client to speculate. I understand, Detective Inspector, that last night you entered my client's premises without a warrant and, after an incident involving a firearm, you arrested six men known to be involved in international organized crime. It seems their fingerprints were found all

163

over the door of the vault. Is it not possible that they might have been responsible? Or are you suggesting that my client, with no previous criminal record of any kind, is a more likely suspect than six known felons?'

'What about the gun?' demanded Ash. 'Why were you in possession of a gun, unlicensed and illegal, if you aren't part of a violent organized-crime syndicate?'

Caroline put a restraining hand on Ludo's thigh before he could answer. 'With regard to the gun, it had belonged to Mr Slater of the Slater Gallery. As you'll be aware, Mr Slater was murdered and the gallery was closed down. Not knowing how to dispose of the weapon, his traumatized reception-ist asked my client if he would take it away, which he did, intending to hand it over to the police at the earliest oppor-tunity. You arrested him while he was away on a business trip and before he had a chance to do so.'

Banerjee strove to find some way of getting de Coleville to trip up without this woman scuppering it. While he was think-ing, Jack decided it was time to tackle chummy again about the arson. This time they might catch him on the back foot.

'Do you remember being shown these photographs, Mr de Coleville?' He pushed across the photos they'd taken from Parker's laptop, showing Ludovic breaking in and hiding what looked like paintings under a sheet.

'Yes. We've already been through all this. I explained what happened.'

From her reaction, Caroline Jackson clearly didn't know anything about the alleged arson. She pulled the photographs towards her.

'Tell us again, please sir,' demanded Bugsy.

Ludovic sighed impatiently. As I told you before — and might I suggest somebody writes it down, this time — the gallery had become overfull with works of no consequence. I needed to store them somewhere close by until I could pass them on next day to a lesser gallery that handles such items. I knew the shack was empty after the owner died, so I put them in there, temporarily, and I secured it with a padlock.

Unfortunately, some vandals chose to break in and burn it down before I could move the items on.'

'Did you know that Vince Parker was in there when you set fire to it?' Bugsy demanded.

'No, of course not and I keep telling you, I didn't burn anything down. There was no one in there when I stored the paintings.'

'The blowtorch that was used to light the petrol was stolen from a takeaway on the same night that you were in there, buying food.' Bugsy was determined to nail him. 'We have evidence of your credit card payment.'

'Me and a hundred other people! The place is always heaving. It could have been anyone. Probably one of the vandals that set the fire.'

Caroline interrupted. 'DI Dawes, this is a separate line of enquiry altogether. It is not related to the arrest for which we are here and I haven't been able to take instructions from my client. He has nothing more to say at this time. Either charge him or let him go.'

And so it went on, with Ash and Jack trying to extract some kind of confession from de Coleville and Caroline Jackson effectively shutting them down. Eventually, it became clear to everybody, that any evidence the police thought they had, was purely circumstantial. They had to let him go without charging him.

After they'd gone, Bugsy was clearly peeved. 'You know what, guv? If we're not careful, the bugger's going to get away with it.'

'I agree,' said Ash. 'We'll have to do better than this. That solicitor, she's remarkably well-informed. She knew all about our unofficial raid on the de Coleville Gallery and the debacle that followed. She's also right about the fingerprints on the vault door. The six men had been trying to get it open when they were disturbed by Mrs Dawes, her assistant and the Chief Super's wife, who shot at them.' He grinned. 'Feisty lot, your ladies, aren't they?'

* * *

Once outside, Caroline and Ludovic went to the nearest bar and he ordered a bottle of Chardonnay. She poured herself a large glass. 'I saw the report in the *Echo* about that market stall burning down with someone inside.' She looked him in the eye. 'Ludo, did you set fire to it?'

'Well, yes. But I didn't know that seedy little private eye was in there at the time — I swear, Caro.'

She believed him. 'Why the hell did you even admit to putting the paintings in there? I saw the photos they had. That figure in black could have been anyone and the registration number of your car wasn't visible. They might know it was your car, but they couldn't have proved it. Why didn't you come to me when all this started?'

'I wish I had now. You were amazing. Do you fancy dinner tonight?'

She smiled. 'You have no moral compass at all, have you?'

CHAPTER TWENTY-SIX

Corrie was getting ready for bed. She wasn't one for endless pots of night cream, but she did look after her complexion to the extent of slapping on a bit of moisturiser. Jack was sitting up in bed, reading the *Richington Echo*, while he sipped his whisky nightcap. He sniggered.

'Corrie, come and look at this. There's a photo of you and Cynthia Garwood taken at last year's police dinner dance. The front-page headline reads: *Kings Richington's modern-day Thelma and Louise.*

'Bloody cheek! We didn't kill anybody.'

'It says: *Mrs Cynthia Garwood — alias Louise — shot a man who was attempting to rape Mrs Corrie Dawes — alias Thelma.*'

'That's not true. They make it sound far more lurid than it was. Cynthia shot the bloke in the ear by accident and it was Carlene he was molesting.'

Jack sniggered again. 'A bit further down, the editor writes: *Following the incident, the Coleville Gallery looked like the aftermath of a Butch Cassidy and Sundance shoot-out, with bullets peppering all the artefacts.*'

Corrie snorted in disgust. 'I'd like to pepper *his* artefacts! Where does he get his information?'

'Where does the *Echo* usually get its information? The Kings Richington grapevine picks up half a story from someone who knew a woman, whose hairdresser heard it from a bloke, who was in the pub next door when it happened — then the editor makes the rest up. Blimey, the old man isn't going to like this next bit. *Mrs Garwood is the wife of George Garwood, a Chief Superintendent in the Metropolitan Police. The* Echo *understands that the police will be taking no further action against Mrs Garwood.*'

'Is there any actual news in that rag?' wondered Corrie.

'Course not. People don't buy the *Echo* for news, they buy it for sex and scandal. They're not bothered whether it's fake or not.'

Corrie changed the subject. 'I thought we'd have a barbecue this weekend. We all need to calm down a bit.'

'OK. Who are we inviting?'

Corrie chewed her lip in thought. 'Bugsy and Iris, her son Dan and his family, George and Cynthia, and I thought it would be nice to invite Ash Banerjee.'

Jack screwed up his face. 'Have I got to do the barbecue?'

'No, Carlene and Antoine are cooking the food. It's going to be a French-inspired barbeque, apparently.'

'So — frogs' legs kebabs, snail burgers and sausages made from pigs' guts.'

'Don't be silly, darling. Sometimes, I think being married to a chef hasn't taught you anything at all.'

'Are you sure we should invite the Garwoods?' asked Jack.

'Oh, yes. My thinking is that if we invite them, it might quash the rumours about my food giving her garden party food poisoning. I mean, if you really believed a caterer had poisoned your guests, you wouldn't accept an invitation to go and eat their food, would you?'

'No, I suppose not. Shall I have another whisky or are we going to sleep?'

Corrie climbed into bed. 'No, and yes. Night-night.'

* * *

It was perfect barbecue weather. Carlene, with her leg heavily bandaged, was chirpy as ever. She and Antoine had got ahead of the game and prepared marinated steaks, chicken and sausages, ready for the grill. Sardines, squid and langoustines languished on a warm tray, alongside an oozing camembert. Antoine had made tabbouleh, which, although North African, was frequently served at French barbecues. Jack tasted it and pulled a face. The combination of mint, bulgur wheat, spring onions, olive oil and lemon juice was a bit much, in his view.

Corrie thought it delicious. 'Jack, you have the taste buds of an ailing kitten.'

'Much more of that and I shan't have any taste buds at all.'

Salads were waiting in the fridge and different kinds of bread were warming in the oven. It was something of an experiment, as the couple was thinking of adding various types of international cuisine to their repertoire. French food seemed like a good place to start, as Antoine was already accomplished. The Garwoods and Ash arrived together.

Corrie greeted them. George and Ash went across to where Jack was dispensing drinks. For Corrie, it was something of a luxury to be hosting a get-together dressed in something smart, instead of emerging from a hot kitchen with limp hair and wearing an apron. For once, she didn't feel upstaged by Cynthia, in her floaty frock.

'I'm so glad you could come. How are you, Cynthia?' They air-kissed.

'I'm fine now, Corrie, thank you. Georgie says in view of the circumstances, I probably won't get five years for discharging a firearm in a public place and wounding two bystanders, a water cooler and Lord Nelson. It's to do with possession and intent, apparently. The gun wasn't mine and I never intended to hurt anybody. There'll be an enquiry, of course. Is there wine?'

'Sunshine wine, Mrs Garwood.' Carlene limped over with a glass of chilled rosé. 'I know we Brits associate pink wine with women who get birthday cards with high heels and handbags on 'em, but Antoine says in France, every bugger drinks it — including men.'

Bugsy and Iris arrived then, with her son Dan, his wife and two children. There was a cheerful buzz of conversation as everyone temporarily forgot art fraud, organized crime and arson. Even the food-poisoning cloud that had been hanging over Corrie had lifted. Bugsy went across to the barbecue, where Carlene and Antoine were creating appetizing aromas.

'Right, young Carlene. Where's the grub? I haven't eaten since breakfast and me stomach thinks me throat's been cut.'

She grinned. 'Now, you've got to be a bit adventurous today, Sergeant Bugsy. No pork pies, pasties or sausage rolls.'

'Might I suggest *merguez* in a baguette with some salad nicoise?' Antoine offered, in perfect English.

Bugsy looked at the long, thin, alarmingly red beef sausages with heavy doses of paprika and garlic, sizzling on the grill. 'Have you got something a bit less . . . er . . . aggressive?'

'Try some Toulouse sausage, Monsieur Bugsy. It's less spicy.'

Bugsy peered at it. 'Is that the one curled up like dog poo?'

Carlene laughed. 'Here, Sergeant Bugsy. This is your kind of nosh — *une côte de boeuf et pommes de terre frites*.' She handed him a loaded plate.

'Now, that's more like it — good old steak and chips.'

George Garwood was talking to Ash about the haul of forgeries they had confiscated, and the six men in custody. 'Good work, Detective Inspector Banerjee. It will look impressive on your record.'

'Thank you, sir. But I should point out that DI Dawes and his team contributed considerably to the success of the operation. He deserves much of the credit.'

Yes, thought Garwood. *Bloody Jack Dawes. He's done it again, hasn't he? Come up smelling of roses, despite ignoring proper procedure.* There was something about Dawes that made Garwood uncomfortable, put him at a disadvantage, made him feel inferior. He'd have him transferred, if he wasn't worried that the successful, clear-up rate of the MIT would suddenly plummet. That was down to Dawes and Sir Barnaby knew it.

'Good. Glad we could assist,' he growled.

'Of course, it would have been even better if we could have nabbed the guys at the top of the food chain. Unfortunately, Rob Slater, the man who might have helped with that, is dead. I'm glad to see that Mrs Garwood is fully recovered from her ordeal.'

'Yes, Cynthia's fine.' George was still smarting from the report in the *Echo*.

Dr Dan Griffin had been playing cricket on the lawn with his kids. Hot and perspiring, he went across to where Jack was dispensing proper drinks. Despite Antoine's assurance that it was indeed a man's drink, pink wine wasn't to everybody's taste.

'Jack, do you think I might have a word? I didn't want to talk shop at your barbecue, but we don't see each other very often.'

Jack handed him a cold beer. 'Of course, Dan. Is something wrong? It isn't Iris or the family, I hope.'

'No, nothing like that. Everybody's fine.' He frowned. 'I just wanted to run something past you. It's probably nothing, but you know what police officers and doctors are like — always looking for ulterior motives or hidden symptoms.'

'Yep, we're a suspicious lot.'

'I've certified a couple of deaths recently — a man and a woman. Nothing violent or fishy, it was a cardiac arrest in each case. I'd been treating them both for heart problems, so I was able to sign them off without a post-mortem. It's just that despite their conditions, and in the case of the man, a very unhealthy lifestyle, I hadn't really expected either of them to die just yet. I did suggest to the woman's son that a post-mortem might clarify the exact heart issue that killed her, but he wouldn't hear of it. Said nobody was going to chop up his mother out of idle curiosity, so as there was nothing discernibly untoward, I couldn't insist. Obviously, you can never be certain how long a patient with cardiac disease will live, but a doctor usually has a rough idea. As a police officer, what do you think? Am I being unnecessarily pedantic?'

'Not at all. If that's your gut feeling, you shouldn't ignore it. I never do and you'd be surprised how often it turns out to be right. Tell you what, why don't you send the details of the two deaths over to my office? I'll take a look at the circumstances, very discreetly, there'll be no suggestion of a breach of confidentiality. If I don't find anything, at least it'll put your mind at rest.'

'Thanks Jack. I'd be grateful. I didn't want to bother Mike with it in case he thought I was taking advantage of him being Mum's fiancé.'

It still amused Jack to hear Bugsy referred to as Mike because even though that was his name, he'd been Bugsy for as long as anyone could remember.

* * *

When Jack received the details of the two deaths from Dr Griffin, he realized that he had come across them both. Jericho was the elderly Rastafarian who had run the colourful Jamaican stall down the end of the Kings Market. The reggae music that pulsated from it was compelling. Even Jack had felt the urge to jig about to the rhythm when he'd walked past. He'd seen other stalwarts of Kings Richington surreptitiously doing the same. Corrie had been shopping at the market the day Jericho had staggered out and collapsed in the street. Both she and Carlene had been sorry to see him go. According to his health records, he drank too much rum and smoked illegal substances. Uniform had been aware and turned a blind eye, as he didn't deal to anyone and never became disorderly. There were details of his heart problem, but nothing in the file indicated that Dan had expected him to die any time soon.

The other patient was Ida Wilson. She had been in the house when Jack and Bugsy had gone to question her son. Jack remembered Bugsy saying the old lady had a face like a bag of spanners, and her son was probably more scared of her than his interrogation by the police. While he was no expert, Jack could see that Mrs Wilson had been on a fairly moderate level of heart medication before her death, with the option to increase it if her symptoms became worse. Not on death's door, then.

If these were, indeed, suspicious deaths, as Dan thought they might be, the first line of detection was motive. Who would want either of these people dead? Jack knew that Bugsy's first instinct was always to follow the money. He needed someone to do some discreet digging into their financial backgrounds without setting any hares running. If it turned out that both deaths were indeed natural, with no foul play, then there'd be no harm done. He asked DC Fox.

A couple of hours later, she returned with the information. 'Jericho didn't have any money apart from a pension, sir, so no financial gain for anyone after his death. His grandson loved him very much and looked after him as well as he could, but the old gentleman was very independent. His body is being taken away to be buried back home in Jamaica, where the rest of his family live, and no doubt to the accompaniment of his favourite Bob Marley music.'

'What about Mrs Wilson?' asked Jack.

'A different story there, sir. Ida Wilson was minted. Money in loads of different accounts, bonds and other investments, all doing well. Everything goes to her only son, David. She's also going to be buried abroad, in Rome, alongside her late husband. Obviously, much loved by her son and daughter-in-law — she's lived with them since their marriage. The house belongs to David's wife, Mrs Wilson junior. No other children and no grandchildren.'

'Thanks, Gemma. Good work. Would you ask Sergeant Malone to come in, please?'

Jack brought Bugsy up to speed with what he was doing. He'd worked with him for so long they could almost read each other's thoughts, and Jack respected Bugsy's opinion on everything. He didn't always agree with it, but Bugsy looked at things from a different, more global perspective, which was invaluable. A copper could become blinkered over the years. Jack conceded that between them, Bugsy and Corrie provided the down-to-earth grist to his occasionally whimsical mill.

'What are you thinking, guv? There might be another reason they died, apart from a dicky ticker?'

'Dr Griffin just wanted it looked at with a fresh pair of eyes, trained at spotting anything shifty.'

'Iris said she thought both deaths were sudden. She works in the health centre and she said Mrs Wilson used to turn up at all hours, dressed in her finery, without an appointment and demand to see Danny. No indication that she could snuff it at any time, but I guess you can never tell. She looked OK that time we saw her, didn't she?'

Jack nodded. 'The son adored her, apparently. He's gone to no end of expense to have her buried in Rome, next to his father.'

'He can afford it, can't he, now he's getting all her loot? Maybe he decided to bump the old girl off, while he's still young enough to enjoy the money. Maybe he put arsenic in her tea.'

Jack looked pensive. 'What did you make of the daughter-in-law?'

'Can't remember much about her, really,' replied Bugsy. 'She's the kind of woman who blends in with the wallpaper — mousy, nondescript, what Iris would call a neutral personality. Why, what did you make of her?'

'I detected an undercurrent,' said Jack. 'How would you feel about your mother-in-law living with you, right from the day you were married? Did you notice, when we were there, how the old girl ordered her about — and in her own house? Told her to get out of the way and go and make tea.'

Bugsy frowned. 'You see, guv, I don't pick up on all this touchy-feely stuff, like you do. But now that you mention it, there was a kind of atmosphere. But would she go as far as bumping her off? And if so, how?'

'There were no injuries and Dr Griffin put the cause of death down to acute myocardial infarction,' said Jack.

'If Danny said she died of a heart attack, then she did,' agreed Bugsy. 'But I guess we don't know what caused it, do we?'

'And don't forget, the son was playing away with the de Coleville woman. I doubt if the wife knew about it, but I'm pretty sure the mother did. He said there was nothing we couldn't say in front of his mother. She might even have been condoning it. That would add to the bad feeling, for sure.'

'Jack, you missed your vocation, mate. You should have been a trick-cyclist or a social worker.'

Jack laughed. 'I don't think so. I have enough trouble trying to guess what Corrie's thinking, never mind sorting out a stranger.'

'What do you want to do, then?'

'There isn't much we can do for poor old Jericho — he's already on his way back to Jamaica. As for Ida Wilson, we don't have any evidence that her death was anything other than from natural causes. David Wilson flatly refused to allow a post-mortem on his mother, even though Dr Griffin suggested it would give him a clearer idea of why her heart gave out when it did. And now Wilson's had her embalmed, apparently.'

'In that case, would a post-mortem tell us anything anyway?' Bugsy wondered.

'Why don't we have a word with Dr Hardacre?'

'OK, guv. Big Ron will have all the answers.'

* * *

Dr Hardacre was hosing down her autopsy table, which was swimming in blood. She stopped when she saw Dawes and Malone push open the swing doors.

'Gentlemen, this is an unexpected pleasure. Do I have one of your unfortunates in my mortuary for slicing and dicing?'

'Not at present, Doctor. I wonder if we might ask you a hypothetical question?' said Jack.

She held out her arms for her assistant, Miss Catwater, to pull off her rubber gloves. 'Certainly, as long as you won't mind a hypothetical answer.'

'Is it possible or feasible to perform a post-mortem on a body that's been embalmed?' asked Bugsy.

She raised her bushy, black eyebrows. 'Strewth! You haven't got Tutankhamen outside in your police van, have you, Sergeant?'

Bugsy reckoned that was as close as Big Ron got to making a joke. 'We're not sure exactly what effect the process would have on a body, where cause of death might be, for example, poisoning.'

Dr Hardacre peeled off her scrubs to reveal a nylon petticoat, mercifully long enough to conceal the iconic knickers. Miss Catwater helped her into a gown.

'Well, gentlemen, that's an interesting question. During the embalming procedure, the blood is removed from the body through the veins and replaced with formaldehyde-based chemicals through the arteries. The embalming solution may also contain other chemicals, such as glutaraldehyde, methanol, ethanol, phenol, water and dyes, which might skew any findings.'

Bugsy was scribbling furiously. 'Can you slow down a bit, doc?'

'Write faster, Sergeant, I haven't got all day. There's a combine harvester accident waiting outside.' She continued. 'However, a post-mortem can reveal some things that embalming wouldn't cover up, such as any physical trauma. In addition, there can be areas of the body where the fluid can't be fully injected. An elderly person, for example, may have a blocked blood vessel that the fluid didn't penetrate. Whether the toxicology report would reveal any foreign substances, such as poisons, depends on the poison involved and the quantity that was used. However, a good barrister can call anything into question, regardless of the truth, so I'd say unless you have other evidence, a post-mortem wouldn't clinch it.' She beckoned to Miss Catwater. 'Come, Marigold, our farmer awaits, and don't forget the poor fellow's head.'

* * *

'Well, Jack, I don't know about you, but I reckon it's looking bad for Wilson.' They were in the car driving back to the station. 'His mother dies suddenly, when the doctor reckoned she was good for a few more years at least. He's the only beneficiary of a shedload of dosh, he's refused a post-mortem, had the old girl embalmed and he's shipping her off to Italy, before we get suspicious. Gotta be him, hasn't it?'

'Or, maybe she just had a heart attack and died,' concluded Jack.

CHAPTER TWENTY-SEVEN

Ida's body was still in cold storage at the funeral parlour. David had insisted on having her embalmed, so she wouldn't 'go off' during her journey to Italy. Fenella had laughed at that. He'd often called her 'Mummy' — now, she actually was one. She was surprised he hadn't wanted her lying in state in an open coffin, so all her cronies could file past and write totally erroneous eulogies in a book of remembrance. Instead, she'd discovered he was planning to have his mother packed in ice, like an ugly old trout on a fishmonger's slab.

There had been a delay with the flight, which gave Fenella some breathing space in which to plan his murder. By now, she didn't see it as murder — more like squashing an irritating wasp. Humanity, she decided, would be better off without him. And she most certainly would!

* * *

'One more push, Fen, and we'll be home and dry.' Judith and Fenella were serving on the Ladies' Guild stall. 'Now, you know what you have to do? We've been over it several times.'

'I've practised my lines. The hardest part will be telling him that I'm sorry for the way I've behaved, I understand he's missing his mother and that he wants to live abroad. And as for the bit about wanting to part friends . . .'

'I know. Just keep thinking that every cloud has a silver lining, there's light at the end of the tunnel, and any other cliché that gets you through. As soon as he's in bed with his Ovaltine, you come straight to me.'

'He isn't taking the tart with him. I saw the ticket,' said Fenella. 'It's a single, one-way, plus a mummified corpse in an ice-box.'

'I wonder how Sasha feels about that,' mused Judith.

'I doubt if she even knows. She's going to be very disappointed after David's dead and all the money comes to me.'

* * *

Fenella was ready. It was time. David had handed in his notice and was preparing for his move to Italy. He was travelling light, he told her, because he now had enough money to buy anything he wanted, once he arrived in Rome.

'I hope you're not expecting me to give you any of Mother's money, Fenella.' He was packing a few clothes ready for the early start in the morning.

'Of course not, dear. I shouldn't dream of accepting it.' *Because once you're dead, it will be mine — all of it — you miserable, pathetic excuse for a human being!*

'Good, because I feel I'd be letting her down if I did. She never liked you and you went out of your way to hurt her. I know you won't admit it, but I'm sure you did something to antagonize her, the night she had her heart attack. Because I wasn't here, you thought you could torment her.'

If you hadn't been out with your tart, I couldn't have done it! Now for the difficult bit. 'Don't upset yourself, David. You have a long journey tomorrow and you need to be relaxed. You're looking very stressed and tired.'

'Of course I am. What do you expect? I've been through hell, these last days. Now, I have to take poor Mother to an alien country.'

It's Italy, you pillock, not Outer Mongolia and you're never going to get there.

'At least she'll be at peace, lying alongside my dear father.'

You never knew your father. It's just as well. What a disappointment you'd have been. Weedy Wilson! 'I'm so sorry, David. I understand how much you're missing your mother and I really don't mind you going abroad, to make a new life for yourself. I reacted badly at first, but now I can see it's for the best. I hope we can part friends.' *Oh God — I may throw up!*

'Well, all right, I suppose there's no need for unnecessary animosity, now it's all over.'

'Tell you what, why don't you have an early night? Go up and have a nice long soak in the bath and pop straight into bed? I'll make your Ovaltine and bring it up to you.'

'Yes, that would be nice. I'm simply exhausted and I think I'm starting one of my headaches.'

'Off you go, then. I'll bring it up when I hear you get into bed.'

Soon after he'd gone up, Fenella could hear the water running. She poured full cream milk in a saucepan and put it on the hob to warm. Then she took a large mug and put several teaspoons of sugar in it. Outside, she took the container of safe antifreeze and emptied it down the drain, then filled it with Judith's deadly stuff that she'd kept in the boot of her car. She placed it near the back door, ready to put beside the Ovaltine tin, so when they found him, they'd guess what he'd done.

She waited, pacing the hall. This had to work. It simply had to. When she heard the bath water running down the plug hole, she mixed up the fatal concoction, stirring it well, so that all the sugar dissolved. Then she took it upstairs. David was in bed.

'Here you are, dear. Drink it all up while it's warm.' She imagined that's what Ida used to say to him, when he was little. 'I'll go away now and leave you to sleep.'

He hesitated. 'Just a minute, Fenella. Don't go yet.'

Please God, she thought. *He isn't going to suggest a reconciliation, is he? Or even worse, ask me to kiss him goodnight, like Mummy used to.*

'I need to taste it, first, to make sure you've made it properly. You know what Mother used to say about your poor food preparation.'

One more word, thought Fenella, *and I won't need the ethylene glycol — I'll brain him with the bedside lamp.*

He sipped it, delicately, like a fussy little girl. 'Yes, that's all right. You can go now.'

She looked at him one last time, remembering all those years of relentless humiliation, the cruel criticism and abuse she'd put up with. The number of times he'd sided with his mother when he should have supported his wife. His stark refusal to use a sperm donor because "the baby wouldn't be Mother's grandchild." The evil old matriarch was dead and her precious son would soon be joining her in hell.

She smiled at him. 'Goodbye, David.'

She hurried down to the hall, where he left his briefcase, and took out his mobile phone. *Don't switch it off*, Jude had said. *It will look suspicious.* Nobody was likely to phone him at this time of the evening. She took it into her bedroom and hid it in her knicker drawer. Then she fetched the container of ethylene glycol and placed it on the worktop, beside the tin of Ovaltine and the used milk saucepan. You didn't stop to wash things up when you committed suicide. She looked around. Everything was as she and Jude had planned. Time to go.

Her car was parked in the drive, a small Fiat Uno that Judith had found for her. It already had her overnight bag in the boot. She grabbed her handbag and keys and slipped out.

* * *

'You're shaking, love.' Judith pulled her into the kitchen and sat her down. She poured her a brandy.

'I've done it, Jude. Exactly like you said. I didn't forget anything.' She looked at her watch. It had taken her half an hour to drive out to the bypass and Judith's flat. 'Will he be dead by now, do you think?'

'Was he drinking the stuff when you left?'

'Yes. He tasted it to make sure I'd made it properly.'

'Then if he isn't already dead, he will be very soon. Now, it's crucial we get the next bit right. Remember, you've been here since lunchtime. You and David had argued over his plan to fly his mother's body to Italy. He was very depressed and wanted to be left alone, so you came here to spend the night with your best friend, to give him some space.'

'In the morning, I go back home and find him dead. Shocked and horrified, I dial 999 and the police come. You'll be with me, won't you, Jude?'

'Of course I will. We'll tell the police that you phoned me as soon as you got home and found your beloved husband dead and I drove straight over to comfort you. Now, I'm going to cook you some supper. It's what we'd do normally. We must behave exactly as we would, if we didn't know David was dead.'

* * *

David took another sip of his Ovaltine. Well, at least Fenella had got that right. It was very sweet, just what he wanted, as he would have a tiring day tomorrow and he'd need the energy. He was looking forward to it. Not burying poor Mother, of course, but a whole new life ahead of him. He wouldn't marry again, he'd decided. He was still young — relatively. He'd have a good time, now he wouldn't be forever having to referee arguments between his wife and his mother. Very tiresome. Why Fenella always had to be so confrontational, he would never understand. He blamed that butch girlfriend — she put her up to it.

It was quiet downstairs. He couldn't hear the television. She must have gone to bed already. He'd get moving early in the morning — he didn't want any embarrassing scenes or floods of tears. A clean break, that was the way to do it. He'd decided that, on second thoughts, he would give his solicitor instructions to instigate divorce proceedings and draw up a new will as soon as he'd gone. Once he had set up a bank account in Rome, the money could be transferred.

He was about to gulp down the rest of his Ovaltine, when he heard his phone ringing. He'd set up different ringtones for his contacts, so he'd know who was ringing and whether he wanted to answer. This was the one he had for Sasha. He looked at the clock. Ten thirty. What on earth did she want at this time of night? He decided to ignore it. He hadn't told her he was going abroad tomorrow and he wouldn't be back. He saw no reason why he should. It had been fun while it lasted, his little dalliance, but it was over now and he was moving on. After a minute or two, it stopped. He picked up his mug of Ovaltine.

Damn! He could hear it ringing again. She was quite capable of going on like this all night. It might be simpler if he just answered it and fobbed her off until he was out of the way.

He got out of bed and was about to go down to get his phone from where he always kept it, in his briefcase, when he realized the sound was coming from Fenella's room. Why had she taken his phone? Who knew? She'd been behaving strangely for some time now. He went into her room, expecting to see her in bed, but it hadn't been slept in. He traced the continuous ringing to a drawer in her dressing table. He opened it and with some distaste, he unearthed his mobile from under a pile of her knickers.

'Hello? Sasha? Why are you ringing me at this late hour?'

He could hear her breathless, husky voice, that he'd once found so sexy. 'David, darling, I have some wonderful news.'

'Yes? What is it?' He didn't imagine for a moment that he would find it wonderful, but she wouldn't go away until she'd told him.

'No, I don't want to tell you on the phone. It's too important. I want to see your face, when you know.'

'All right. I'll ring you tomorrow and we'll arrange to meet.' He'd be long-gone by then.

'No, now! It has to be now — right away.'

'For goodness' sake, Sasha, I'm in my pyjamas. You surely don't expect me to get dressed and come out to meet you now.'

'You'll be glad you did, I promise. I'll meet you at the gallery. It's been cleaned up and I know the security settings. We can be private there.'

'What about your husband?' David certainly didn't want any chance meeting with de Coleville. The man was a brute and a bully.

'Ludo's at home in the house, consulting with his solicitor. He won't bother us.'

'Oh, very well. I'll meet you at the gallery in half an hour.' He turned off the phone, thinking he may as well get it over with or he'd never get any sleep. He got dressed then looked longingly at his Ovaltine, getting cold with a skin forming on the top. He'd heat it up in the microwave when he got back.

Downstairs, on his way through the kitchen, he saw the container of antifreeze on the worktop. What on earth was it doing there? Fenella must have been messing about with it, but why she needed antifreeze in June, he couldn't imagine. Something to do with that peculiar friend of hers, who owned a garage. No job for a woman, in his opinion. Those things are best left to men, who know what they're doing. He took it back out to the garage and put it on the shelf, where it belonged. On his way out, he noticed Fenella's car had gone. She'd be cosying up with the girlfriend. Fine, best she was out of the way. It would make parting easier when he left in the morning.

CHAPTER TWENTY-EIGHT

Ludovic de Coleville opened a second bottle of Veuve Clicquot with an expertise that chimed with his debonair image.

'Am I in the clear, then, Caro?'

Caroline Jackson crossed her legs revealing a tempting, if subtle, amount of thigh. 'Maybe not entirely, yet, but we're getting there. The police don't have any real evidence against you, except for the gun. The mandatory minimum sentence is five years' imprisonment, but the offence is to possess a firearm with intent to endanger life. We can prove, with evidence from Monica What's-her-name, that you only possessed it briefly, at her request, to take it out of harmful circulation. Your intention was to give it up to the police. You haven't any previous, and you don't look like Al Capone, so with a bit of luck, we can pull off a suspended sentence.'

Ludo refilled her glass. 'Whatever I'm paying you, darling, it's not enough.'

'You haven't seen my bill, yet. More importantly, Ludo, I'm trusting that you don't have any more dubious art and antiques hidden away.'

He put a hand on his heart. 'Absolutely not, I swear.'

'And you're not planning to take possession of any in the near future?'

'Nope. I've learned my lesson. I don't want to end up like poor old Rob.'

'Then the only question that remains to be answered is whether they can prove you're guilty of manslaughter as a result of an unlawful act — namely, arson. You've admitted, unwisely in my opinion, that you stored what you called "paintings of no consequence" in that shack, but you've denied setting the fire. You swore you didn't know there was someone in there.'

'That's the truth, Caro. How was I to know? Why didn't the man say something, when I went in?'

'From the pathology report, he was unconscious but not dead, when you doused the place with petrol and set fire to it. We stick to your story, Ludo. There's nothing to be gained by admitting to anything else — not ethically or legally. Now pour me some more champagne before it gets warm.'

* * *

Sasha was waiting on the steps of the recently restored Coleville Gallery when David pulled up in the Lexus. As soon as he got out of the car, she ran to him and threw her arms around his neck. He pulled back and looked around, warily. He'd never been comfortable with public displays of affection. It was one thing to kiss your mother in front of people, but not a girlfriend.

'Sasha, please. You don't know who might be looking.'

'Darling, I don't care. I'm so happy.' She took his hand and led him inside. 'Come with me, my love. I want to show you something.' She took him up to the top floor of the gallery, which housed sculptures of varying appeal and value. One section was labelled 'Religious Art' and contained a collection of Madonna and Child sculptures and paintings. It reminded David of a similar display he'd seen in the Uffizi Gallery in Florence, when he'd visited with his mother as a boy. His enduring memory was that he'd never seen so many po-faced women and fat, ugly babies in his life.

'Sasha, what's this all about? I really want to go home to bed. I'm very tired. I've had a lot on my plate, what with Mother passing away so suddenly. I'm really not in the mood for games.'

She stood close to a particularly ugly sculpture of a pregnant Virgin Mary. The sculptor clearly believed expectant women were shaped like a butternut squash.

'Can you see the resemblance, darling?' she gushed.

David was confused. He'd always considered Sasha a little overeffusive but surely she didn't imagine herself to be a reincarnation of the Madonna? 'No, I'm sorry. I don't know what you're talking about.'

'That's me,' she squealed. 'I'm pregnant with our baby. Isn't it wonderful?'

Whatever David had been expecting, it wasn't that. He snorted. 'Of course you're not. It's impossible.'

'No, it isn't, sweetheart. We've made love loads of times and never taken any precautions. It was bound to happen.'

David really didn't need this charade. Were all women determined to call into question his ability to breed? 'Sasha, if you're pregnant, it most definitely isn't mine.'

'But it is, my precious. How can you doubt me? I haven't been with anyone but you for months — well, weeks, anyway.' She was becoming tearful.

'Sasha, this is ridiculous. I'm going home. I have a long day tomorrow. I'm taking my mother to Rome to be buried next to my father. And incidentally, I'm not coming back.' He thought she may as well know. It would put an end to this farce.

'What? No! David, darling, what are you saying? You can't abandon me, especially now I'm having your baby. You have to take me with you. Ludo is divorcing me. I can't stay here on my own. I don't have any money.'

'You'll find someone else and I'd do it soon, if I were you. A woman's sexuality is a rapidly diminishing asset.'

'But we were planning to get married and have babies. We could set up home in Rome, if that's what you want. I'll have our baby there. It will be wonderful — lots of sunshine, wine, music, pasta . . .'

David was starting to lose patience. 'Sasha, you are *not* pregnant by me — that's if you're pregnant at all, which I doubt. I'm unable to father children. What were you planning to do? Leave it a few weeks, until I was completely fooled, then tell me you'd had a miscarriage? It won't wash, I'm afraid.'

Sasha face turned white with anger. 'I'm the one who's been fooled. You pretended we were going to get married and have a family, when you knew all along that it could never happen. This is the second time we've been engaged, and you've let me down — just like you did the first time.'

'Don't be silly. We weren't engaged, it was just a few nights in a hotel because I was irritated with Fenella. If you thought it was anything more, I'm sorry, but trying to trick me into marriage is underhand and deceitful. If I hadn't known I was sterile, I might have fallen for it. Now, I'm going home, and I suggest you do the same.' He turned to walk away.

'Don't you dare turn your back on me!' Sasha rushed at him, furious. 'I hate you!' She pounded on his chest with her fists and clawed at his face.

David was taken completely by surprise. He abhorred physical violence of any kind and tried to fend her off. It turned into an angry scuffle, until she gave him one last, fierce push. He lost his balance and staggered towards the balustrade. The two-hundred-year-old wood, that had long been in need of renovation, cracked under his weight and splintered. Sasha watched in horror — it almost seemed like slow motion — as David hurtled thirty feet to the ground. His terrified shrieks and the dull thud, as his body hit the hardwood floor, would haunt her dreams for ever.

She ran down the staircase and knelt beside him. His eyes were still open and a pool of blood was slowly spreading under his head. With trembling hands, she took out her phone and dialled 999.

'Police? You'd better send someone to the Coleville Gallery. I think I've killed my fiancé.'

* * *

It was something after two in the morning when DI Dawes's phone rang. He sat up and put on the bedside light, trying not to wake Corrie.

'Guv? It's me. We've got a suspicious death, possibly murder — uniform have just phoned it in. They're attending the scene.'

Jack ran fingers through his tousled hair. 'Bloody hell, Bugsy. Why can't people arrange to get bumped off during social hours? Where is it?'

'You're not going to believe this, Jack. It's the Coleville Gallery.'

'That place must be cursed. Who's our unfortunate corpse?'

'You're not going to believe this, either. It's David Wilson.'

'Not the same David Wilson that we interviewed about the arson? You reckoned he'd offed his mother for her money.'

'The very same, and you won't believe who made the 999 call.'

Jack sighed. 'Bugsy, old friend, if it's you that's telling me, then I'll believe it, won't I.'

'Sorry, guv. It was Sasha de Coleville — his bit on the side. According to uniform, she reckons she shoved him off the second-floor balcony. Big Ron and her crew are already there.'

'OK, I'm on my way.' He turned off the phone.

'On your way where?' mumbled Corrie from under the duvet.

'There's been a suspicious death at the Coleville Gallery.'

'Has Mr de Coleville killed Mrs de Coleville, or vice versa?'

'Neither. The deceased is David Wilson.'

Corrie sat up. 'Not Fenella Wilson's husband? Dear me, poor woman. First her mother-in-law, now her husband. She must feel like she's surrounded by death.'

Jack thought about that for a moment. 'You could well be right. Go back to sleep, I'll see you in the morning.'

* * *

Dr Hardacre was kneeling beside the corpse examining his skull, which had cracked open like an egg. There was now a sizeable pool of blood. She looked up as Jack and Bugsy approached.

'Well, here we are again, gentlemen. Pretty straightforward. He fell from up there.' She pointed up at the shattered balustrade. 'Landed on his head, poor devil. He might have survived, if he'd absorbed some of the shock with his legs or landed on his side, then rolled. As it is, he'd have died as soon as he hit the floor. Broken neck and fractured skull.'

'Any indication that he was pushed?' asked Jack.

'No obvious signs of violence. I'll tell you more when I've done the post-mortem, but it doesn't look as though he sustained a punch hard enough to send him through the balustrade. More likely he lost his balance, fell against it and it gave way.' She sniffed loudly. 'This place should have been pulled down years ago. Full of dry rot and decay — you can smell it.'

All Bugsy could smell was Big Ron's personal brand of perfume — formaldehyde. 'You don't believe listed buildings should be preserved, then, doc?'

She looked up at him witheringly. 'I'm a scientist, Sergeant, not an historian. This building was ugly when it was built in 1810. It hasn't suddenly acquired appeal because it's old, and it's obviously dangerous and no place for members of the public.' She addressed Jack. 'I understand you know the deceased. His possessions are with the SOCO team, but his phone was still in his pocket.' She handed it over in an evidence bag. 'It survived the fall rather better than its owner.'

Back outside, Jack looked at his watch. 'It's early but I suppose we have to give Mrs Wilson the bad news, before she finds out from someone else. You know what the grapevine's like in Kings Richington.'

'That's going to be a jolly conversation. *Guess what, Mrs Wilson? Your husband's dead. He was shoved off a balcony by his mistress.* Talk about adding insult to injury.'

'Call Gemma Fox and ask her to meet us at the Wilsons' house. It's always advisable to have a female officer available on these occasions.'

When they arrived, it was clear there was no one home. They knocked a few times, but the house was locked up and there were no cars outside. Uniform had reported that David Wilson's Lexus was still parked outside the gallery.

'We ought to find her, sir,' said Gemma. 'Pretty grim if the first she knows about it is when she reads it in the *Echo*.'

'You're right, Gemma. The death message has to come from us.'

'Have we got her phone number?' asked Gemma.

'We can't tell her over the phone,' said Bugsy.

'No, I meant we could find out where she is, then ask her to come home, as we need to speak to her.'

Bugsy thought not. 'Best we go and see her. If she gets the wind up, drives like a mad woman, then gets killed in a crash, we'll have wiped out the last member of the Wilson family.'

'Shall I ring the station, sir, see if they can trace her number?' asked Gemma.

'No need,' said Jack. 'We still have David Wilson's mobile.' He pulled it out of his coat pocket, still in a plastic envelope. 'As long as it isn't locked, we should find her mobile number on it.' He fiddled with it for a few moments.

'Let me, sir,' said Gemma. 'I have a phone like that. It's easy when you know how.' She pressed a few keys and handed it over. 'There you are, sir.'

'You ring her, Gemma. It'll be less of a shock if she hears a female officer's voice.'

Bugsy was trying to remember what Fenella Wilson looked like. She hadn't made much of an impact on him when they were in her house interviewing her husband. All the same, it was going to be an unpleasant experience for her. He wondered if she had anyone to look after her, afterwards. If not, they'd have to get a Family Liaison Officer.

'Mrs Wilson? I'm Detective Constable Fox from the Metropolitan Police. I'm sorry to call this early in the morning, but it's very important that we talk to you. If you give me the address of where you're staying, we'll come straight over. No, I'd rather not discuss it on the phone, if you don't mind.' She paused. 'Yes, I know where that is. We'll be there shortly.' She turned to Jack. 'She's in a flat over Kelly's Car Services and Repairs — a garage on the bypass.'

'I wonder what she's doing there?' said Bugsy.

'Maybe she's got a boyfriend. After all, her husband had a mistress,' reasoned Gemma.

'Nah. She didn't look the type,' said Bugsy.

'What does the type look like, Sarge?' asked Gemma.

Bugsy sensed he was drifting into shark-infested waters. 'Shall we go? Don't want to keep the lady waiting.'

CHAPTER TWENTY-NINE

Fenella was making coffee in Judith Kelly's tiny kitchen. Her hands were shaking and she spilled the sugar.

'What exactly did she say?' asked Judith.

'That she was a police officer and needed to speak to me urgently. Oh Jude, do you think they've found David?'

'How could they? The plan was that you'd call them after you got home this morning and found him dead. They'd have no reason to go to your house otherwise. And even if they did, how would they have got in? You locked up after you left, didn't you?'

'Yes, of course I did.'

Judith mulled it over. 'David wouldn't have been able to let them in. He'll be stiff and cold by now.'

'So why does she need to speak to me?' worried Fenella.

'Who knows? It could be anything. And even if they have found David already, would it matter? They'd come to the same conclusion, that he'd made himself a mug of Ovaltine and laced it with antifreeze, while deranged with grief over the death of his mother. Don't panic, Fen, it'll be all right. You're in the clear because you've been here with me, since yesterday afternoon.'

'Have I? Oh yes, of course. I'd forgotten.'

'Fen, pull yourself together. You have to stick to your story. They'll establish the time of death was around ten thirty last night. You weren't there. You were here. Have you got that?'

'Yes, I think so.' The doorbell rang and she jumped.

'Stay here, I'll let her in.'

Judith was surprised to see a deputation of three officers, but she didn't show it. 'Please, come in. Mrs Wilson is through here.'

'Before we speak to her, may I ask if you're a relative, madam?' asked Jack quietly. 'Only I'm afraid we have some bad news for Mrs Wilson and she'll need someone to stay with her. I can arrange for a police liaison officer if that would be better.'

'No, I'm Mrs Wilson's best friend. I'll look after her. Has there been some kind of accident?'

'In a manner of speaking. Her husband, David Wilson, fell from a balcony in the Coleville Gallery, last night. He died instantly.'

Judith swallowed hard. Her mind was racing. What had gone wrong? What the hell was the bloody man doing there, when Fen had left him in bed at ten thirty, drinking a mug of poisoned Ovaltine? Somehow, she needed to warn Fen, before she said something incriminating and it all went tits up. But it was too late, the fat copper was in there already.

'I'm so sorry to be the bearer of bad news, Mrs Wilson.' *Blimey*, thought Bugsy, seeing her ashen face, *the poor soul looks traumatized already and I haven't told her anything yet*. 'I'm afraid your husband was found dead last night. I'm sorry for your loss.'

'Oh my God,' wailed Fenella. 'I knew he was dreadfully depressed and miserable after his mother died, but I didn't think he'd do this.'

Judith was desperately trying to catch her eye but Fenella was sticking to the script.

'Didn't think he'd do what, Mrs Wilson?' asked Jack, puzzled.

'Commit suicide. That's what you said, wasn't it? That David had poisoned himself? I've been here with my friend since yesterday lunchtime, so I couldn't have had anything to do with it, could I?'

Oh, Fen, begged Judith, silently. *Don't say any more.*

'Why do you think your husband poisoned himself, Mrs Wilson?' asked Bugsy.

'Well, that's what happened, wasn't it?' Fenella was confused. 'Didn't you say you found antifreeze in his Ovaltine?'

'No, madam, we didn't mention anything about antifreeze or Ovaltine,' confirmed Jack, watching her reaction.

'Then the young lady must have told me, on the phone.'

Jack turned to Gemma. 'DC Fox, did you mention anything about antifreeze or Ovaltine, when you phoned Mrs Wilson earlier this morning?'

'No, sir. I just said it was important that the police talked to her and I couldn't discuss the matter on the phone.'

Fenella finally caught Judith's fraught expression and realized she'd gone too far. 'Well, David kept saying he was unhappy enough to commit suicide and that if he did decide to do it, he was going to poison himself with antifreeze. I just assumed that's how he died. Was he still in bed, when you found him?'

'We went to your house to speak to you at around four o'clock this morning, Mrs Wilson, but there was nobody home,' said Bugsy. 'We didn't go inside.'

She was panicking now. 'I don't understand. If you didn't go in and find his body, how do you know he's dead?'

Jack decided it was time to tell her. 'Your husband fell from the top floor of the Coleville Gallery, around eleven o'clock last night. He was involved in a scuffle and there was an accident. He died instantly.'

Fenella completely lost it. 'He was with that woman, wasn't he? I might have known he'd sneak off to see her, the minute my back was turned. You'd have thought he'd have stayed in bed at that time of night, especially when he believed he'd be flying to Rome today, with his putrefying mother. That was never going to happen!'

Judith was sitting with her head in her hands.

'When did you last see your husband?' asked Bugsy.

Fenella was hysterical. 'I told you, half past ten last night, when I took him his Ovaltine in bed. Why do you keep asking me the same questions? Jude, help me! What do I say now? I feel faint.'

'DC Fox, fetch Mrs Wilson a glass of water. Then I think we need to take her down to the station to make a statement.'

'Are you arresting her?' asked Judith.

'Not yet,' said Jack, 'but I'll have to, if she doesn't come voluntarily.'

'It was all my idea, you know,' Judith declared. 'Fen's life was a living hell. I had to do something.'

'Then I think you'd better come down to the station, too, madam.' Bugsy took her arm.

* * *

They were taken in separate cars and, when they reached the station, put in separate interview rooms. Sasha de Coleville was in a third room, making her statement about the episode at the gallery.

DCS Garwood strode into the incident room. 'What's going on, Dawes? The station's full of women detainees. There's one in each of the interview rooms. Have you been dragging them in off the streets?'

'No, sir. They're all connected to one victim — David Wilson. His wife is here on suspicion of attempted murder. Her friend is here under joint enterprise and his mistress is here, explaining how she came to shove him thirty feet over a balustrade to his death.'

'Popular bloke, then?'

'Yes, sir. And we have the embalmed body of his mother in the morgue, awaiting someone to take responsibility for her.'

196

'Well, you'd better get on with it, man. Should be easy enough to sort out. I'd do it for you, but I have a meeting with Sir Barnaby. Keep me updated.' He strode back out.

'Flippin' cheek,' said Bugsy. 'We'd never get a result, if it was down to old George. The lab's come back with the report on the mug of Ovaltine that forensics took from David Wilson's bedside table. Bloody good job he never drank it or he'd have been dead before Mrs de Coleville had a chance to kill him.'

Jack grinned. 'Bugsy, sometimes you don't even make sense to me and I've known you for donkey's years.'

'It was ethylene glycol, apparently. The real nasty stuff that they don't put in the safe antifreeze these days. I bet it came from Judith Kelly's garage. Who do you want to interview first?'

'Mrs Wilson, I think. She virtually confessed when we picked her up. She may claim she was confused, but she definitely stated she last saw her husband at half past ten on the night he died, when she took him up the fatal mug of Ovaltine. You were writing it down, Gemma. That was what she said, wasn't it?'

'Yes, sir. She's contradicted her original claim, that she left the house at lunchtime and he committed suicide while she was gone.'

'Right, Sergeant Malone and I will handle the interview and you can work the tape machine. I'm all thumbs with those gadgets. Has she got legal representation?'

'No, sir, she said she didn't want it. She asked if her friend could sit in and when I told her that wasn't possible, she burst into tears.'

When they entered the interview room, Fenella Wilson looked strained. She'd been given a cup of tea, which she hadn't touched. Before they could ask her anything, she said, 'Judith has nothing at all to do with this,' she said, before they could ask her anything. 'She knew nothing about it. She's innocent. You have to let her go.'

'Just tell us what happened, Mrs Wilson.' Jack motioned Gemma to start the tape.

'David's mother died of a heart attack. I was cooking her supper when it happened, so David accused me of causing it by not looking after her properly. He was besotted with her — has been, his whole life. We argued. You already know he was having an affair with the de Coleville woman. You came to my home to speak to him about the death of the private investigator, that her husband hired to watch them.' She saw his questioning glance. 'I was listening in the kitchen, Inspector.'

'What happened next?'

'He told me he was taking his mother's body to bury it in Rome and he wasn't coming back. He said he was keeping all the money she'd left him and I wasn't going to get a penny of it, after all the years I'd waited on her and been abused for my trouble. Well, I guess something snapped and I decided to kill him, before he could get away. I put antifreeze in his Ovaltine, then I went out and left him to drink it. I thought when I got back next morning and found his body, I'd phone you and it would look like suicide. The rest you know. But I didn't kill him — his tart did that.'

There were more questions and she filled in more details. Finally, Jack concluded the interview. 'Stand up, please. Fenella Wilson, I'm charging you with the attempted murder of David Wilson. You do not have to say anything, but it may harm your defence if you do not mention . . .'

Norman Parsloe, the custody sergeant, put her in a cell, until she could be processed. She sat down on the bed. *At least*, she thought, *I've got away with the murder of his vicious old mother.*

Judith Kelly seemed fairly resigned to her situation. 'It was all my idea, Inspector. You've seen Fen. She isn't capable of working out a plan like this.'

'Do you see murder as a feat of intelligence, Ms Kelly?' asked Jack.

She shrugged. 'I'd consider this one irrelevant, Inspector. David Wilson *was* irrelevant, in the greater scheme of things. He couldn't even get murdered with any panache. He died in a sordid brawl with his mistress. He won't be missed by anybody. How much more irrelevant can you get than that?'

Bugsy explained that she would be charged with attempted murder under joint enterprise. She didn't argue.

Norman took her away and put her in a cell. 'You planning on keeping the third lady, Jack?' he asked. 'Only it's getting a bit full down here, what with the two ladies who have to be kept apart and the six blokes waiting for Border Enforcement to come and sort them out.'

'Don't know yet, Norman. We're just going to interview her.'

According to DC Aled Williams, who had been tasked with taking her statement, Sasha de Coleville was 'like a tit in a trance.'

'Honestly, sir, I think it's only just hit her, what actually happened.'

'But she's well enough to be questioned?' asked Bugsy.

'Yes, Sarge. In fact, she wants to get it over with and go home. I asked her if she wanted a solicitor and she said no, she didn't, and she especially didn't want Mr de Coleville's solicitor, because he was sleeping with her and she would probably try to get her banged up for life.'

Sasha de Coleville was, indeed, in a state of flux. Jack and Bugsy went in to question her, with Aled managing the tape machine and taking notes. She stood up, as soon as they entered.

'Can I go home, please? I've told this officer everything that happened.'

'Just a few questions, madam,' said Jack. 'Please sit down.'

She sat, reluctantly.

Jack and Bugsy had read through her statement. 'You say here, Mrs de Coleville, that you phoned Mr Wilson and asked him to meet you at the gallery. It was late at night. What was the urgency?'

'Ludo had been beastly to me, saying he was going to divorce me and I shouldn't get any money, as the gallery and the house were both in his name. I was desperate. David and I were lovers — engaged again, actually.'

'Had you been engaged to him before?' asked Bugsy.

'Yes, before either of us married, but he broke it off and I married Ludo.'

'OK, so you went into the gallery and you took him up to the top floor, to show him a sculpture of the Madonna and Child.'

'That's right. I told him I was pregnant. It wasn't strictly true but I was sure I would be, before long. He didn't believe me, said I was trying to trap him. But we'd planned to marry and have babies. He'd told me he wanted children but his wife didn't. It was a lie. He was actually a — what do they call it? — a Jaffa, seedless. He tricked me.'

'You say here,' said Jack, 'that he told you he was going to Italy to live, but without you, and you got angry.'

'Yes, I did. First Ludo dumping me and now David. I lost my temper. I flew at him and he stumbled backwards. Then the balustrade snapped and he fell over the edge. I never meant to harm him — I loved him.' She began to cry. 'Why are men so horrid to me?'

'You called the police straight away?' asked Bugsy.

'Yes, of course. I could see he was dead. I didn't know what else to do. What will happen to me, Inspector?'

* * *

Outside, Bugsy shook his head. 'Blimey, guv, her lift doesn't go all the way to the top, does it, poor cow.'

'What will she be charged with, sir?' asked Aled.

'Not really for us to decide, said Jack, 'but my guess would be involuntary manslaughter; an unlawful death but without the intent to kill or cause serious harm. There's culpability, obviously, but it wasn't a pre-meditated crime, it was a spur of the moment thing. Not too far from being an accident.'

'She'll get a suspended, most probably,' said Bugsy. 'Christ, what a day. Is the pub open?'

CHAPTER THIRTY

When Ludovic found out that Sasha had been arrested and was in police custody, he thought she must have pinched something — probably frilly knickers from a lingerie boutique. It wouldn't occur to her to pinch something expensive, like one of the designer handbags she kept buying that cost him a fortune. He wondered whether he should ask Caroline to go to the station and find out what was going on. It wouldn't look good for business — a kleptomaniac wife — and whether he liked it or not, she was still his wife until Caro had sorted out the divorce situation. Eventually, he decided against any involvement. He was keeping a low profile. Thanks to Caro, the heat was off temporarily regarding the forgeries in his vault and the arson. The police had only circumstantial evidence and unless they found something more substantial, he was only looking at a suspended sentence for possession of a firearm.

He was feeling quite carefree as he strolled down Kings Richington high street. It was market day and the stallholders were in full cry.

Strawberries — two for two pounds fifty!

Get your designer jeans here — only eight pounds a leg!

Furry phone cases — not ten, not eight, but five pounds for three! Cost you twenty quid in Curry's!

The fragrance of freshly cut flowers attracted him to the florist's stall. He stopped and bought a generous bunch of lilies with an intoxicating perfume. He would give them to Caro when he saw her that evening. She had invited him to her apartment for dinner. He had already bought champagne — flowers would be the perfect accompaniment. He preened, smoothing back his immaculately styled hair. He was nothing, he thought, if not wildly attractive to women.

He reached the end of the street, pausing on the steps of the Coleville Gallery to pull out his phone and disconnect the alarms. Behind him, he could hear a powerful motorcycle, moving towards him at high speed. *Blasted bikers*, he thought. *Why didn't they stay on the bypass instead of coming into town?*

The engine was still racing when it drew level with Ludovic. As the bike sped past, the pillion rider, in black leathers and a full-face helmet, pulled out a gun and fired.

'What the—' was all Ludovic managed to splutter before he plunged backwards down the steps. The bullet had formed a neat hole, dead centre between his widened eyes, and dropped him where he stood. The lilies he was carrying fell across his dead body like a funeral spray on a coffin.

* * *

'I don't think we've ever had a drive-by shooting in Kings Richington,' announced Bugsy.

'Sign of the times, Sarge,' said Aled. 'It's like Detective Inspector Banerjee says, we're fighting international criminals now. This wasn't so much a killing as an execution.'

'Aled's right,' agreed Ash. 'The mob whose goods we confiscated couldn't allow de Coleville to get away with what they saw as a double-cross. They lost a sizeable stash of valuable merchandise and six of their foreign operatives. This was a message to others they do business with that misdemeanours will be summarily dealt with.'

'No chance of catching who did it, I suppose?' asked Jack.

'Not a scooby, guv,' said Bugsy. 'Loads of CCTV cameras, showing two blokes dressed from head to foot in biking gear, faces concealed by helmets, on a stolen bike found burned out on the common. They'll be miles away by now.'

'They're nothing if not professional,' said Mitch. 'Dr Hardacre's report, together with ballistics, say it was a perfectly targeted shot, delivered at speed, and de Coleville would have been dead before he hit the ground.'

As if on cue, the door opened and Dr Hardacre walked in with Miss Catwater in tow. 'DI Dawes, might I have a word?'

'You can have several, Doctor. You know you're always welcome in our den of murderous iniquity.'

She ignored that. 'It's to do with the embalmed body of Ida Wilson in my mortuary. Now that there are no longer any objections from the family, I obtained permission from the coroner's office to perform a post-mortem. What prompted my curiosity was the mug of Ovaltine laced with ethylene glycol that the daughter-in-law proposed to administer to her husband.'

'Doc, didn't you say the embalming solution may also contain other chemicals, that might skew any findings?' asked Bugsy.

'I did, Sergeant, but I also said that there can be areas of the body where the embalming fluid can't be fully injected. That an elderly person, for example, such as the late Mrs Wilson, may have a blocked blood vessel, which the fluid didn't penetrate. This was, indeed, the case.' She held out a hand to Miss Catwater. 'Marigold, the tox report, if you please. Once we had a clue what poison to test for, we were able to find it. Mrs Wilson had ingested a considerable quantity of ethylene glycol, which brought on her heart attack. But it's a particularly vicious substance which, if it doesn't stop the heart immediately, causes kidney failure. As enzymes break it down, a chemical reaction creates calcium oxalate crystals, which concentrate in the kidneys and neatly slice the cells apart.'

'Nasty,' observed Bugsy, grimly. 'It would have killed the old lady anyway.'

'In my opinion, yes, Sergeant. It would simply have taken a little longer.' She turned her attention to Jack. 'Inspector, in view of the same poison turning up in both Mrs Wilson's corpse and in Mr Wilson's Ovaltine, I thought you may find the coincidence worth investigation — but of course, that's for you to decide. I merely offer the evidence. Good day.' With that, she swept out, with Miss Catwater trotting to keep up.

'What do you make of that, sir?' asked Gemma. 'D'you reckon the two women did away with the old lady?'

'It's beginning to look like a possibility,' agreed Jack.

'Motive?' asked Mitch.

'Follow the money,' said Bugsy, predictably. 'We knew there was tension in that household, down to the constant presence of David Wilson's domineering mother, and his affair with Mrs de Coleville. Ms Kelly told us Fenella Wilson's life was a living hell.'

'They hatch a plan to bump her off, only to find that after she's dead, David Wilson is planning to leg it to Italy with all the loot,' said Aled.

'The obvious solution is to murder him too, then all the money goes to the wife,' said Bugsy. He looked at Jack, deep in thought. 'You're quiet, guv. What are you thinking?'

'I'm thinking about something Dr Griffin said regarding an elderly Jamaican gentleman with heart problems, but who wasn't expected to die so soon. Gemma, didn't you say you were at university with his grandson, Desmond?'

'That's right, sir. He studied Politics and Philosophy and I studied Law. We used to joke that he was going to end up as Prime Minister and I was going to be a High Court judge, Ms Justice Fox, DBE.'

'And here you are, slumming it with us lot,' grinned Aled. Gemma grinned back and threw a ball of paper at him.

'Do you think Desmond would spare us a few minutes of his time?' asked Jack. 'I'd like to talk to him about his granddad.'

'I'm sure he would, sir. I'll give him a ring.'

* * *

Jericho's grandson, Desmond Bailey, was happy to talk about his grandfather, whom he had obviously cared about a great deal.

'You see, Inspector Dawes, he was something of an iconoclast. He had a home and family in Kingston and used to travel back regularly, especially for the reggae concerts, during Bob Marley week. But for some reason, he would never go home for good. He liked the UK and enjoyed being part of the Kings Market.'

Jack nodded. 'He was well loved here, too. The market traders say it isn't the same without Jericho's stall and the Caribbean music. Were you aware of his heart problems?'

'Well, yes, but he never thought it important. The doctor gave him regular checks and he was under mild medication, but we didn't think it was serious. That's why it was such a shock when he died suddenly.'

'One last thing, Mr Bailey. Did you know your grand-dad was fond of rum and smoked weed?'

Desmond smiled. 'He did have an unhealthy lifestyle, but as I said, he was an iconoclast — a rebel. I used to buy his rum, he liked the sweet, treacly, over-proofed Jamaican stuff, but obviously' — Desmond winked — 'I had nothing to do with his ganja.'

Jack winked back. 'Of course not, Mr Bailey. Do you know if he left the rum unattended behind his stall?'

'Oh, yes. Granddad wasn't the type to lock anything up. He knew how to relax and enjoy life — a quality to be aspired to, in my opinion.'

On his way out, Desmond passed Norman Parsloe. He shook his hand and, in perfect received pronunciation remarked, 'Sergeant, good to see you again. Keeping well, I trust?'

* * *

'I know what you're thinking, Jack.' Bugsy fetched them both coffee and doughnuts from the canteen.

'I'm thinking you'd better not tell Corrie I've been eating canteen doughnuts. She says they're just dollops of badly cooked dough.'

Bugsy bit into his and covered his chin with sugar. 'You're thinking that someone laced Jericho's rum with ethylene glycol.'

'It would explain why he died earlier than Dr Griffin expected,' agreed Jack.

'It would also explain why Nosy Parker was unconscious in Jericho's shack when de Coleville torched it. I reckon he went in there to see what de Coleville had hidden, drank some of the rum, and passed out.'

'You're a mind-reader, Bugsy. But what I can't work out is . . .'

' . . . the motive.' Bugsy lifted up his tie and licked jam off it. 'Why would anyone want to poison Jericho?'

'Exactly. There was a clear motive for Mrs Wilson and Ms Kelly to want to do away with Ida Wilson and David Wilson but not a harmless old market trader.'

'Maybe it was a dummy run, guv. Perhaps they weren't sure how much would be fatal or what the symptoms were.'

'The Ladies' Guild stall is in clear view of Jericho's,' recalled Jack. 'It would have been easy enough to slip some antifreeze in his rum when he wasn't there, then watch what happened. I think we need to speak to both of the suspects again. Firstly, regarding the results of Dr Hardacre's post-mortem on Ida Wilson, then about Jericho's rum.'

'Right, and no "Mister Nice Policeman" this time. They're pretty evil, these two.'

'I agree. We police officers can't always be sensitive, caring and diplomatic. Sometimes, we're just woodentops.'

* * *

Due to a backlog of cases awaiting process, Fenella and Judith were still being held in the cells at the station. Dawes decided they should speak to Judith Kelly first, since she had claimed to be the brains behind the attempt on David Wilson's life. She was put back in an interview room, with DC Fox working the tape.

Bugsy went straight in. 'Ms Kelly, how would you respond if I told you that a post-mortem on Ida Wilson revealed large quantities of ethylene glycol in her system?'

She eyeballed him. 'I'd say you were lying. Her son had her embalmed. A post-mortem wouldn't reveal anything. There'd be too many chemicals in the body.'

'On the contrary, there were pockets that the embalming fluid didn't reach and those pockets were full of toxic antifreeze. A search of your premises has revealed that this substance came from your garage. Were you supplying Fenella Wilson with ethylene glycol, to enable her to kill her mother-in-law and then her husband?'

'No comment.'

'What about Jericho?' Jack took over the questioning. 'Did you or Fenella Wilson go into his shack when he wasn't there and lace his rum with ethylene glycol?'

'No comment.' These coppers weren't as dumb as she thought. They had it all worked out.

'You do understand, Ms Kelly, that if Mrs Wilson is found guilty of murder, you will get a similar sentence under joint enterprise?'

'No comment — and I'd like a solicitor now, please.'

* * *

The custody sergeant accompanied Fenella to the interview room, without telling her what was happening. When the door opened to admit the two detectives, she sensed the game was up. She and Jude were not going to get away with just attempted murder. She was weary, now, wanting it all to be over. She hadn't been able to eat or sleep. Her nightmares were peppered with flashbacks of Ida's twisted face, risen from the dead and cursing her. She could still smell her vomit and the soiled nightdress.

Jack motioned to DC Fox to start the tape and began the interrogation. 'Mrs Wilson, how would you respond if I told you that a post-mortem on your mother-in-law revealed large quantities of ethylene glycol in her body?'

She looked at the two men without really seeing them. 'I'd say it's because I put half a pint of it in her sherry and she drank it. I watched her die, then called an ambulance. She was a vicious, manipulative hag and she ruined my life and my marriage for fifteen years. She deserved to die. Will that do?'

Dawes and Malone exchanged glances. 'Do you know anything about the death of Jericho, another stallholder on the Kings Market?' asked Bugsy.

She looked saddened. 'Yes. We were sorry about that. We never intended for him to die. We had to practise, you see. Jude wasn't sure how much of the poison to give Ida to make sure she died straight away, so she put some in Jericho's rum while he was at lunch. Only a bit, but he had a bad heart and it killed him. Can I go back to my cell now, please? I'm so tired.'

Jack formally charged her with the murder of Ida Wilson and the murder of Jericho under joint enterprise with Judith Kelly. He asked her if she understood.

'No, not really, but I'm sure you know what you're doing.'

As she was being led away, she suddenly turned back.

'Inspector, will you apologize to your wife for me? It wasn't her food that poisoned those ladies at Mrs Garwood's garden party — it was my jam. You see, my first attempt at killing Ida was when I put ethylene glycol in her strawberry jam, but she didn't eat it and it subsequently found its way onto the Ladies' Guild stall. I have since discovered that Mrs Garwood bought it and it caused all her guests to be sick. Please tell Mrs Dawes and Mrs Garwood I'm sorry.' She followed the custody sergeant out.

The three police officers looked at each other in something approaching disbelief.

'Sir, is it possible for someone to be intrinsically immoral with no concept of right or wrong and very little remorse?' asked Gemma.

Jack scratched his head. 'If it is, I think we've just interviewed two of them.'

'What will they get?' Gemma wondered.

Bugsy shrugged. 'As far as the Wilson woman is concerned, a good brief might claim she's unfit to plead, worn down by years of bullying by her husband and mother-in-law. Either that, or they'll get a trick-cyclist to claim she's on some kind of spectrum suffering from a disorder that some clever bugger invented yesterday and that nobody's ever heard of.'

'You're such a cynic, Sergeant,' said Jack, 'but it wouldn't surprise me.'

'I don't know about Kelly, though. I reckon they'll throw the book at her,' said Bugsy.

* * *

Back in the incident room, the team was tying up loose ends and preparing reports. The door flew open and DCS Garwood strode in.

'Was anyone intending to provide me with an update, before Sir Barnaby sees the end-of-month budget deficit and closes us down? I realize this is an investigation team but investigations are, at some point, intended to provide results. Correct me if I'm wrong, Inspector Dawes, but we now have four men dead, two women charged with attempted murder, another of involuntary manslaughter, a drive-by execution and six gangsters awaiting deportation. Even with your talent for attracting crime, that's a little excessive for one station. It seems to me that there has been a great deal of expensive fannying about, largely resulting in a commendable achievement of bugger-all.'

'On the contrary, sir,' explained Jack. 'We have admissions of guilt to two murders, an explanation for the arson and the charred private eye and here's the really important bit — we know who poisoned the jam that Mrs Garwood gave to her charity ladies. It calls for a press release to the editor of the *Echo*, don't you think?'

* * *

That evening, Jack arrived home with flowers from the market and two bottles of elderflower wine.

Corrie looked at them suspiciously. 'What have you done? Tell the truth and I promise not to draw blood.'

'Harsh — very harsh,' said Jack. 'I haven't done anything, only that with which you tasked me, Oh light of my life — namely, proving it wasn't your catering that poisoned Cynthia's tea party.'

'Oh, Jack, have you really? That's amazing. I mean, business hasn't been too bad, but I'm sure there's still some reluctance to risk my food. It's understandable.'

Jack opened one of the bottles of wine. 'Do you remember when you, Cynthia and Carlene were doing your snooping and you suspected the culprit was a jar of strawberry jam?'

'Yes, but we gave up on that because we decided you couldn't be poisoned by jam — Carlene did the module.'

'Maybe not, but you can if someone has laced it with ethylene glycol.'

'But who would do a thing like that and why, for goodness' sake?'

'You went to see the woman who made the jam — Fenella Wilson?'

'Yes, we did. President of the Ladies' Guild and a perfectly nice woman, we thought.'

'She and her girlfriend put poison in the jam, intending to kill her harridan of a mother-in-law. Instead, it found its way onto the market, Cynthia bought it and the rest, you know. They also put some in Jericho's rum as a trial run, to see how much would kill. Eventually, they put half a pint in the mother-in-law's sherry and that finished her off. Fenella Wilson's husband was going to be next, but his mistress pushed him over a second-floor balustrade, before he could drink it.'

Corrie was speechless, for a nano-second. 'My God! Who'd have believed it? What sort of mind is evil enough to think up such wicked things?'

'The murderer's mind — and that, Corrie, is the dark side of the moon.'

EPILOGUE

FENELLA WILSON AND JUDITH KELLY

Fenella Wilson and Judith Kelly were each handed down two life sentences, to run concurrently. After a lengthy trial, the jury did not accept the defence counsel's claim that Fenella Wilson was 'under a mental disability' when she committed the offences — specifically, the murder of Ida Wilson, the murder under joint enterprise of Jericho and the attempted murder of David Wilson. The judge found that the defendant was 'of sound mind and discretion, had killed unlawfully and that she had been sure that death was a certainty, as a result her actions.' Judith Kelly's counsel made no attempt to plead extenuating circumstances and she accepted the judge's ruling without demur.

Initially, they were sent to separate women's prisons but due to overcrowding, they were transferred and eventually, to their joy, found themselves sharing a cell. During work periods, Fenella taught art classes and Judith serviced the prison vehicles. Although it wasn't what they had envisaged when they planned to live together, it made 'life' seem much less punitive.

SASHA DE COLEVILLE

Sasha de Coleville was found guilty of involuntary manslaughter. The court recorded that the defendant had no previous convictions and had expressed remorse. With the focus on a low culpability factor, it was deemed that there had been no intention to kill or cause grievous bodily harm, and the judge accepted that there had been a high level of provocation. In addition, she had recently become widowed. She received a six-month sentence, suspended for a year.

Once the Health and Safety Executive was alerted to the unsafe condition of the Coleville Gallery and the cost of putting it right, it was considered to be under threat. It was taken over by the National Trust as a building of national importance, due to its historic interest.

Sasha sold the country mansion on the Thames and went to live in Spain, where she caught the eye of a wealthy, middle-aged Marqués. She soon became his Marquesa and bore him four children in rapid succession. All memories of Ludovic de Coleville, David Wilson and Kings Richington were erased from her mind, as if she had pressed a delete button in her brain.

IDA AND DAVID WILSON

Ida Wilson's body was cremated in the Kings Richington Crematorium with no pomp and ceremony and no mourners — not even the ladies from Laburnum Lodge. David Wilson's corpse was similarly dispatched. The cost of the simple incinerations was paid by David's solicitor from the large inheritance he had received following his mother's death.

The forfeiture rule states that a murderer cannot inherit from the deceased person they have killed. This also precludes an individual from benefitting as a consequence of the killing, which was the case pertaining to Fenella Wilson. Since there were no other beneficiaries, the remaining sum, which was considerable, passed to the Crown via the Treasury Solicitor.

THE SLATER GALLERY

When probate was granted in respect of Rob Slater's will, Monica discovered that he had left the Slater Gallery to her. After the initial shock had worn off, she decided to abandon the conceptualist art theme, which she had never appreciated. Instead, she displayed paintings of Tuscan vineyards and Italian lakes, and pieces of colourful Murano glass from Venice. Vivaldi's mandolin concertos plink-plonked softly in the background. Satisfied that she'd had neither knowledge of nor involvement in Slater's art fraud business, the mob left her alone.

THE RICHINGTON ECHO

The press release from the police communications office stated that investigations had revealed the source of the alleged food poisoning incident, and those responsible had been arrested and charged. It was expected that prison sentences would follow.

Another communication informed the editor that the story printed recently, speculating on the cause of the food poisoning, was erroneous and some of the accusations he had published about Coriander's Cuisine were bordering on libellous. Fearing punitive litigation, the editor hastily printed a retraction. In a front-page article, with a full-length photograph of Corrie standing outside her premises, he extolled the virtues of the catering company and its excellent reputation and apologized for any misinformation.

CARLENE AND ANTOINE

Chez Carlene had attracted the attention of Michelin. The notification said that taking into account the high-quality produce, chefs with a mastery of culinary techniques, the taste of the food, the savoir faire and a consistently excellent dining experience, the bistro was duly awarded a Michelin star.

Carlene was so thrilled, she could hardly speak, which for her, was a first. Needless to say, Corrie was immensely proud. On the back of the recent retraction, she suggested to the editor of the *Echo* that he might want to give the bistro a centre spread. The resulting increase in diners meant hiring two more staff.

CYNTHIA GARWOOD

Cynthia Garwood was elected president of the Inner Wheel Club of Kings Richington. She liked to think it was because of her popularity, her ability to promote friendship and embrace the ideal of service with the added dimension of personal concern. In reality, she knew it was because of her central role in what was being called the 'Great Gallery Gunfight.' No matter. She had beaten Lady Lobelia Featherstonehaugh, whose only claim to fame was the ability to projectile vomit into a pond.

DI JACK DAWES

During Detective Chief Superintendent Garwood's annual performance review, Commander Sir Barnaby Featherstonehaugh suggested that the time had come for Dawes to be promoted to DCI. It was apparent that much of the success of the MIT was down to him. Garwood had responded that he didn't think Dawes was ready for promotion yet. He was too prone to acts of spontaneity and frequently ignored PACE guidance. Added to which, thought Garwood, his transfer to another division would throw his own shortcomings into stark relief. No, it was never going to happen on his watch.

BUGSY AND IRIS

In a tiny chapel in rural Richington Parva, guests gathered to witness the wedding of Michael 'Bugsy' Malone, bachelor, and Iris Emily Griffin, widow. Bugsy wasn't what he called a 'God-botherer,' but he knew a church wedding was important to Iris and for her, he would do anything. Her son, Dr Dan Griffin, gave her away and her grandchildren, James and Olivia, acted as pageboy and bridesmaid.

Jack Dawes was Bugsy's best man — a role he thought he would never play — but he was proud to be there, supporting the man he could trust with his life. Bugsy was the epitome of honesty and loyalty and he was also a good bloke to have on your side when the going got rough.

Afterwards, the small but exclusive reception was catered by Corrie and Carlene, who alternated between laughter and tears for most of the day. The superb haute cuisine buffet included some pork pies, pasties and sausage rolls, reflecting Bugsy's impeccable taste in food.

THE END

ALSO BY FRANCES LLOYD

Made in the USA
Middletown, DE
16 May 2024

54378049R00132